The Assassin
Galveston

Jim West

ISBN
Hardcover: 978-1-965134-03-0
Paperback: 978-1-965134-02-3

Page Left Blank Intentionally

Other books by Jim West

DNAlien
DNAlien II
DNAlienIII
Genocide by GMO
Living Within a Strange Mind Volume I
Living Within a Strange Mind Volume II
The Making of an Assassin Atlanta
The Assassin Baltimore
The Assassin Chicago
The Assassin Denver
The Assassin El Paso
The Assassin Fort Worth

My special thanks go once again to one of my most extended friends (you'll notice that I didn't say oldest), John Fleenor. Tirelessly, he plows through my incoherent ramblings and tries to make sense of the nonsensical with a sharp wit and more than a few snide comments about my writing skills.

Thanks, John. You've done well. Again.

Page Left Blank Intentionally

Chapter One

Jim Lashley had just finished the last three-day trip for the month, flying for American Airlines. After telling the crew goodbye, he boarded the small tram that carried him to the employee parking lot.

As he approached his airport car, actually a rather unremarkable ten-year-old double cab pickup, he hit the remote button to unlock the doors. Tossing his roll-a-board suitcase in the rear seat, he stood motionless beside the front door, contemplating the next ten days until his first flight of the upcoming month.

Finally opening the door and climbing in behind the wheel, he started the engine and realized that he dreaded going home. It had been over six months since he had avenged his wife Jennifer's death at the hands of the men who had been intent on assassinating him.

Her death, now over a year and a half ago, and his long, painful rehabilitation still haunted him. Every step in the house seemed to echo with loneliness. The phantom aches from the numerous bullets that had ripped into his muscles, broken bones, and shattered teeth never abated.

The everyday mundane things like the smell of early morning coffee brought back haunting memories of what he had lost. Had it not been for his longtime mentor and friend, retired Marine General Gene Barker, he doubted if he would have made it this far without falling out of society.

If he hadn't met the General in Vietnam while serving his second tour as a mud Marine on a Long Range Recon Patrol team, Jim's life would have never arrived at this point. It was Gene who got Jim into the program to become an officer, a Marine F-4 pilot, and later a pilot for American Airlines.

It was while attending the Marine Aviation Cadet (MarCad) program at Pensacola Naval Air Station, Florida, that Jim met Jennifer. After their marriage and the end of the Vietnam War, the General had him transferred to a Marine Reserve unit and brought him into the Black Water family.

Before being hired by American Airlines, Jim used his deployment with the Marines to execute numerous highly controversial assignments for Dark Water, the clandestine enforcement arm of Black Water's international operations.

Once a pilot for American, he was transferred to Muddy Water, the domestic enforcement arm of Black Water. It was because of his association with Black Water, and more specifically, Muddy Water, that he was targeted by a rival corporation that was trying to compete for extremely lucrative security contracts.

Now, after twenty years of having Jennifer in his life, Jim was struggling to fill the void left by her death. And General Gene Barker was the only person who got a glimpse into the shell that he had become. The rage that had burned fiercely while he exacted his revenge on the men who had killed his wife no longer provided a reason to continue.

Always a man who confronted each obstacle head-on, he found no way to face this current problem, no solution to the constant loneliness that seemed to shroud every waking moment. The more he tried to find a spark of happiness in his life, the more it seemed to evade him.

Knowing just sitting in the parking lot wasn't a solution, Jim started his pickup and headed for the airport exit. As he left, heading south to join 183 eastbound, he reluctantly headed home.

Joining I-35 as he neared Dallas, he grew even more apprehensive. His options for the next few days were unlimited, but he couldn't see any that might provide the least bit of satisfaction.

Before Jennifer's death, they would have relished such free time. Now, it seemed almost a curse to Jim.

As he maneuvered to take I-30 eastbound, the only thing that seemed logical right now was to find some quiet place and lose himself in a couple of drinks.

Exiting Highway 80 down to the 635 loops, he tried to think of someplace where he hadn't been with Jennifer and, therefore, might not be filled with memories.

Taking the exit for Scyene Road, he soon saw the sign for the local VFW ahead on the left. Pulling in, he removed the epaulets from his white shirt and tossed them along with his tie into the passenger seat.

Seeing only a few cars this early in the evening hopefully meant few people inside. Right now, a conversation with a stranger was not what he desired. Just time to sit and reflect was all he wanted. The less human contact, the better.

Chapter Two

After ordering a Ziegen Bock beer from the bartender, he glanced around at the room and opted for a table toward the rear of the bar. Sitting with his back to the wall, Jim noted the few men sitting at the bar along with one lady who was the only female other than the bartender.

The interior was pretty standard for every VFW he had ever been to. The usual neon beer signs, more signs of the branches of service, and a scrolling sign noting it as VFW Post 8785 adorned the walls.

Moments later, a couple walked in and ordered beers before coming back to one of the pool tables near where he was sitting. Muttering under his breath, Jim looked for another place to sit, but this was as far from the couple or the people at the bar as he could get.

Almost halfway through his beer, he saw the door open, and a familiar figure walked in and glanced around. Spotting him sitting alone, Gene smiled slightly and headed over.

"Little early for a beer, isn't it Marine?" Gene said as Jim stood to greet him.

"The sun's over the yardarm, isn't it, General?" Jim answered, shaking Gene's hand.

"Guess that would depend on your latitude, wouldn't it?" Gene replied as he glanced at the couple playing pool.

"My latitude? More likely my attitude," Jim told him, motioning for him to take a seat.

"And how's that coming?" Gene asked as the bartender approached.

"Varies," Jim answered. "Only half past dead is normally a good day."

"Would you like something, sir?" the bartender asked, looking at Gene.

"I'd love a Ziegen Bock, young lady," Gene told her. "And another for my friend here, if he's ready."

Jim nodded and said, "I'll be ready by the time you get back, ma'am."

"So, only half past dead?" Gene mused as they waited for the bartender to return. "Hell, that's at least a little improvement. The question is if you're half past dead, heading toward dead, or coming back from the dead?"

"Haven't quite figured that out yet," Jim replied, smiling. "Some days, I have a difficult time knowing which way I'm going."

"I'm sure you'll get a handle on it," Gene told him as their beers arrived, and he handed the bartender a twenty-dollar bill.

"Cheers," Gene then said, picking up his bottle. "To those that go swimming with bowlegged women."

"Cheers," Jim replied, tapping the neck of his bottle against Gene's. "And to that philosophically astute sailorman, Popeye! But I believe his phrase was swimming with bald-headed women."

"You are correct," Gene responded as he sat back and watched the pool players for a couple of moments and then observed, "That's not what I'd call a normal pair for a mid-afternoon pool game at a VFW."

"You noticed," Jim said, shaking his head.

"Sort of hard not to," Gene replied as the man missed a shot.

"My guess is the guy is some low-level supervisor, and the lady is a new hire single mom, recent divorcee, or widow," Jim said, shaking his head.

"You're probably right," Gene agreed, nodding. "Cheap khaki pants, white socks, Walmart tennis shoes, and a rather snug around-the-gut knit shirt. That's the uniform of the day for a lot of the civilian world."

"Yeah, I figure he's her supervisor, and he's been asking her out for a drink since she got hired," Jim added. "She's probably in her late thirties, maybe early forties, and desperately needs her job. He looks to be in his mid-thirties. Hasn't seen a donut or cheeseburger he didn't like and couldn't find a gym if it was next door."

"You've been in the civilian world long enough to know that's becoming the norm," Gene said. "And unfortunately, the Marines have been seeing much the same issue in their recruiting."

"The airlines just increased the average passenger weight by ten pounds for figuring takeoff and landing speeds," Jim added. "And we're carrying more seatbelt extenders than just a few years ago."

"Does that remind you of anything?" Gene asked, nodding toward the pool table.

"Oh, yeah," Jim answered. "That low-life dipshit who was dogging Jennifer at the office."

"Still have that bottle of skunk scent?" Gene asked, smiling.

"That was just an accusation," Jim answered, smiling as he remembered the incident. "And I was cleared of any wrongdoing."

"And I know what you did," Gene said, trying to hold back a laugh at the memory. "And I'd say the man got off lucky, knowing you as I do."

Chapter Three

"So, what did you fly all the way from Quantico for?" Jim asked, changing the subject. "Certainly not a beer at the local VFW."

"We've got a little project under evaluation down in Galveston," Gene answered, nodding. "The company wants me to take a look at the situation and make a recommendation."

"And I'm going out on a limb here and guessing you just wanted to take me along to help with your evaluation," Jim said, looking at Gene. "And it's my guess that you know I have ten days off and nothing planned."

"I'm not sure of the *nothing planned* part," Gene admitted. "But I am aware of your flight schedule, and I could use your field experience to help me look at what Black Water is being asked to perform."

"And I'll hazard another guess that you located me here shortly after landing at Love Field," Jim added. "Complements of Bracer and her covey of computer nerds."

"She was asked to provide me with your location as I was leaving Love Field," Gene acknowledged. "I certainly didn't want to drive to your house and find you had decided to take a trip or something."

Shaking his head, Jim said, "My life's an open book to the company. How's she doing anyway?"

"Remarkable," Gene answered. "We'll discuss some of the new technology she's been working on while we're in Galveston. That is if you have no previous commitments."

"Only one," Jim told him. "And it's still a couple of days away."

"Oh?" Gene said as the bartender came to check on them.

"Another beer, gentlemen?" she asked, smiling.

Gene looked at Jim and nodded, saying, "Please, but cut us off after that. I can't afford this guy's extensive beer tab, and I know he'll never offer to pay for mine."

"Be right back," she said, turning away.

"So, what's the commitment?" Gene asked, watching Jim closely.

"Sort of a date," Jim finally admitted. "I'm not so sure it's a good idea anyway."

Gene sat back and waited a second and then nodded, saying, "It's about time. But why do you think it's not a good idea?"

"I didn't say I didn't think it wasn't a good idea," Jim countered. "I just said I wasn't sure it was. There's a big difference between the two."

"All right, tell me about this *may not be a good idea* date," Gene said leaning forward and putting his elbows on the table.

"Just someone I met recently," Jim answered as the bartender set their beers down and took the empties.

Gene motioned to the change from their previous beers for the bartender and continued, "And she is …?"

"I never said it was a she," Jim replied, smiling and tapping Gene's beer with his. "You need to stop making assumptions given today's social environment."

"I would bet my pension, and yours, that Jim Lashley would rather join a monastery and take a vow of celibacy before switching teams," Gene said. "I don't consider my question about who *she* is to be an assumption but a well-known fact. Don't forget how far back we go and the secrets I know."

Jim emitted a small laugh and agreed, saying, "The only monastery around here is very selective in their recruitment. You have to take a vow of celibacy just as your father did and his father before him. Very selective group."

"And you continue to evade the answer," Gene replied, shaking his head. "Is there something I shouldn't know?"

"No. It's just a bit early to know if this is the right thing to do," Jim answered. "I'm concerned that I'll be making more comparisons than I should. Maybe I should wait a little longer."

"I think it's time," Gene advised. "And I'm aware of the difficulty of taking the first step, but if nothing else, it gives you someone to go out to dinner with. Go to the movies. Nothing says you have to do anything other than start having a friendship outside of the few people around here you seldom associate with anyway."

"And that's advice from a man that's been alone since when?" Jim asked, knowing the answer.

"Yes," Gene answered. "And that's one of the reasons I offer my advice. I know what living alone for years is. I've lived it. And there are times I regret what might have been. I miss Jennifer. I always will. I miss my wife. I always will. I just want you to take a chance on starting over. Don't let work be your mistress for the rest of your life. Now, tell me about this young lady."

Chapter Four

"I met her at a restaurant," Jim finally admitted. "Italian place just north in Garland."

"Don't tell me you've gone somewhere besides Venice Pizza for Italian food," Gene joked. "Isn't that some sort of cuisine infidelity?"

"I was hungry, the restaurant was there, things happen," Jim answered smiling. "I never intended on what happened. But it was pretty damn good food."

"I'm starting to see a little déjà vu here," Gene remarked, smiling and sitting back. "Maybe not a hamburger joint, but food-related."

"Don't think it didn't occur to me as well," Jim replied, smiling.

"Now, finish the story," Gene said, taking a sip of his beer.

"Well, I just stopped in for a bite to eat a couple of weeks ago," Jim continued. "Small family type place. There were not many cars in the parking lot, but it was still pretty early for dinner.

I was escorted to a table in the back by the owner, a nice guy with a huge mustache. Reminded me of Gusteau in the movie Ratatouille," Jim said.

"Gusteau didn't have a mustache," Gene countered. "Not even a pencil-thin one. Now the food critic, whoever he was, I believe did."

"Actually, it was Chef Skinner who had the skinny mustache. The guy who took over after Gusteau died," Jim corrected him. "But for some reason, that's what I thought of when he led me to the table. Maybe the tall Chef's hat and apron. I don't know. But I half expected to see a little mouse peek around the corner."

"Then what?" Gene asked, smiling at the mental image.

"Then she walked up," Jim answered.

Gene paused for a couple of seconds and then said, "I assume you mean this was the lady you're having second thoughts about."

"Yeah, that was her," Jim answered. "I don't know why she got my attention. There was just something about the way she smiled. It was sort of a twinkle in her eyes sort of thing. It's hard to describe, but that's the first time in a long time that someone has piqued my interest."

Gene had a knowing smile on his face as he said, "I'm assuming you lost a lot of interest in the menu at that point."

"Yep," Jim admitted, smiling and shaking his head. "Took me a couple of seconds to even ask for tea. At least I was coherent enough to say unsweet."

"And gave you a little time to look at the menu," Gene said nodding. "Did you at least have something in mind to order when she returned?"

"Lasagna," Jim answered. "I don't think I even read the menu. Just stared at it until she came back."

"And then you blurted out, 'Can I take you dancing?'" Gene said, laughing. "Maybe, 'Can we go to the VFW and shoot pool?'"

"I hope I've got a little more class than that," Jim said, shaking his head. "And at least I wasn't wearing khakis and white socks."

"You might keep your voice down a bit," Gene leaned forward and said quietly. "And besides, I know you wear white socks."

"Only with my boots," Jim replied, glancing at the couple playing pool.

"All you wear is boots," Gene said. "So, what happened next?"

"She came back with my lasagna and some bread, smiled, and said to let her know if I needed anything," Jim answered. "Nothing except what you'd expect from any waitress."

"And that was it?" Gene asked incredulously.

"No, she came by a couple of times while I was eating and then just sort of wandered over toward the end of the meal and asked how everything was," Jim explained.

"So, I said it was just fine. She smiled and asked if it was '*just fine*?' There was that smile again. I may have said something at that point, but I don't remember."

"So, when did you ask her to come shoot pool?" Gene said, laughing at the image of Jim having a loss for words around a lady.

"A couple of days later, when I went back for dinner," Jim told him. "I didn't exactly go there to ask her out, but that's what happened."

"Speaking of dinner, why don't we drop your pickup off at your house, and you can change into your khakis, knit shirt, and cheap tennis shoes with white shocks, and I'll take you to dinner," Gene suggested, setting his empty beer bottle on the table. "Know any good Italian restaurants up around Garland?"

Chapter Five

After stopping at his house, Jim came out while Gene was still sitting in the black Suburban talking on the phone.

"Ready to head out?" Gene asked, hanging up his call.

"As I'll ever be," Jim answered, getting into the passenger seat.

"Well, you certainly spiffed up," Gene said, smiling and preparing to back out of the driveway. "Starched jeans, starched shirt, clean black hat. A little shine on your Tony Lamas. Guess you're trying to impress someone. Let me guess … by the way, just what is this lady's name?"

"Marie," Jim answered, fastening his seatbelt. "Marie Thompson."

"Thompson doesn't sound much like an Italian heritage," Gene remarked. "Where to?"

"Get back on 635 and head north," Jim directed. "Then we'll take the exit for Shiloh Road and continue north. Follow it for a couple of miles and then make a right on Buckingham Road. Siciliano's A Taste of Italy is where we're going. It's just a couple of blocks east on Buckingham on the right."

"Got it," Gene said as he headed back toward 635. "So, just give me a quick rundown on Miss Thompson so I don't make any faux pas when I meet her. She will be there, I presume?"

"I can't promise you she will, but I think so," Jim answered. "Thompson was her husband's name. He was a cop down in Dallas and was killed in an apparent attack. No one knows for sure if it was random or targeted. Doesn't matter. The fact is, he was shot in the face during a traffic stop."

"What makes you think it was even a hit versus wrong place, wrong time," Gene asked as they entered 635.

"I don't know for sure, but apparently, the dash cam showed the shooter looking directly at him as he sped through a stop sign," Jim told him. "And, the tags were from Louisiana, covered in mud while the rest of the car was clean. And the tags were reported stolen from some small town near Shreveport."

"Ever catch the shooter?" Gene asked as he saw the exit for Shiloh Road coming up.

"Nope," Jim answered as he saw Gene slide over to the exit lane. "Dashcam was too grainy to get any identification of the guy."

"Kids?" Gene asked, making the turn north on Shiloh.

"Twin girls," Jim answered. "Twenty, and both are going to the University of North Texas up in Denton."

"How long ago was her husband shot?" Gene asked.

"Little over two years ago," Jim answered. "I didn't want to press it, you understand. Just pretty much the same questions you just asked."

"What does she know about you?" Gene asked. "How much have you told her?"

"Just that I'm a retired Marine, work for American Airlines, and my wife was killed in a drive-by shooting in

Fort Worth," he answered. "That was probably why she told me about her husband."

"Probably so," Gene said as he looked for the turn for Buckingham Road. "Having a common tragedy is a pretty good opening line. Makes a connection that most people wouldn't understand."

"Unfortunately, it's becoming more common every day," Jim replied as they turned to Buckingham. "Restaurant is just ahead on the right."

"And please don't embarrass me by introducing me as General," Gene reminded him. "You know it's just Gene when we're socializing."

"I remember," Jim said as they pulled into a parking spot. "I assume it's still okay to let her know you were a Marine if she asked. Otherwise, might be difficult to explain our relationship."

"Just stick to the truth if you think you might happen to have somewhat of a chance at a future with this young lady," Gene advised. "Not to say you do or not. But I'm getting the impression that it's a possibility. Even if you're not sure you want to have that first date."

Chapter Six

"Welcome to Siciliano's," a lady said as they entered. "Table for two?"

"I'll take this, Mom," a younger lady said, smiling at Jim and taking the menus. "Jim, I wasn't expecting to see you so soon."

"Unexpected company came into town," Jim said, smiling and removing his hat. "Gene, this is Marie. Marie, my friend Gene."

"Very nice to meet you, Gene," Marie said, leading them into the restaurant. "Table in the rear again, Jim?"

"Please," he answered. "Corner table if possible."

"No problem," Marie told him with a quick glance back at him. "I'll give you our least favorite table. It's the farthest from most of the tables, and being this early, you should have plenty of privacy."

"Thanks," Jim said as she led them to the table.

"What would you gentlemen like to drink?" Marie asked, placing the menus on the table.

"Unsweet tea, please," Jim answered as he took his seat and placed his hat on the empty chair to his right.

"The same for me, please, ma'am," Gene said, smiling with a slight nod of his head.

"Be right back," Marie said, giving Jim a quick smile.

"Don't tell me you don't see it," Gene said quietly as Marie left them.

"See what?" Jim asked, unrolling the napkin with his silverware.

"The obvious similarities," Gene answered, shaking his head. "I swear, she could be a cousin of Jennifer. Maybe a third cousin, but the resemblance is definitely there."

"I don't think you remember what Jennifer looked like," Jim replied, looking at Gene. "It's been a long time."

"Okay, there's a lot that's different," Gene admitted. "And they are major differences. Jennifer was what, five-ten? Marie's probably standing on her tiptoes to be five – two. Hair color, complexion, and other things are distracting the similarities. But her smile and her eyes. I swear she's a miniature Jennifer."

"I don't see it," Jim said, leaning back in his chair. "And I certainly don't see the smile and eye thing." "You're trying to make too much of a comparison of the total," Gene said. "Just look at the smile again. The same quirky little semi-lopsided grin that ends up in her eyes. And the way she looks at you, that's the same look I saw in Jennifer's eyes when I first met her."

"I think you're looking for something that's not there," Jim told him as Marie came toward them with their drinks.

"Here you go, guys," Marie said, setting their glasses on the table in front of them.

"Have you decided on what you'd like, sir?" she asked, looking at Gene.

"Jim mentioned the Lasagna earlier," Gene answered. "I'd like to try that. But only if you'll call me Gene without the sir added."

"My pleasure, Gene. I think you'll be happy with your choice," she said, smiling. "Even though Jim said it was only *just fine* when he had it."

"The man has the taste buds of a bull toad," Gene replied. "You're probably lucky he didn't ask for fried grasshopper. Speaking of fried, do you have calamari?"

"Best in the Metroplex," she answered, picking up his menu. "Shall I add that?"

"Please do," Gene said with a slight bow of his head.

"And you, *Jim, without the sir,* what would you like this evening?" she asked, turning to look at him.

"I noticed shrimp scampi on the menu last time," Jim answered, handing her his menu. "That sounds good."

"Best in the Metroplex," she said as she brushed his hand with her fingers while taking the menu. "Haven't you figured that out by now?"

Sitting back as Marie walked away, Gene crossed his arms and shook his head, saying, "Best in the Metroplex. And as far as you're concerned, probably so. If I was ever sure of something, it's that you definitely need to have that date you're unsure of. I'm sure of it, and I'm seldom wrong when it comes to reading people."

"And just what makes you so damn sure?" Jim asked, sitting back and crossing his arms also.

"Her," Gene answered. "I've learned a lot about you over the years. She's exactly what you need. Hell, she's the same slender type you go for. And don't say you don't. I've had several of our female operatives you've worked with think you might be interested in them. And they all have a slender figure, just like her.

And I knew about your initial infatuation with Jewell," he continued. "Same body type. And the final two pieces of the puzzle … she's already taken with you. And you are with her. I know your look. If there was ever someone who shouldn't play poker, it's you, Jim Lashley. Your every emotion is so plain to see. The only time it's the least bit hidden is when you're focusing on a mission. And even then, it's there. It's just cold and emotionless."

"What about this little issue down in Galveston?" Jim asked as they saw Marie coming toward them. "Can that wait?"

"I'm pretty sure I can arrange scheduling around your previously mentioned commitment," Gene answered. "I know how to prioritize the important things in life. Right now, it's working around what's best for you."

Chapter Seven

After Marie put a basket of fresh baked rolls and butter on the table and walked away, Gene picked one and said, "Here's what we're going to do. You said it's still a couple of days until your date. So, you're going to come with me to Galveston tonight. I've booked rooms for both of us for the next week.

We'll stop by, and you can pack a quick bag and follow me to the airport," he continued as he lathered butter across the steaming roll. "Then you'll have your pickup at the airport when you fly back for your date."

"What exactly are we doing in Galveston?" Jim asked, taking a roll.

"Have you heard of fentanyl?" Gene asked.

"I think so," Jim answered. "Something like opium, isn't it?"

"Yes," Gene said, nodding. "It's a synthetic opioid. It is chemically produced and is an extremely powerful pain relief medication. Its brand name as a prescription is *Duragesic,* and it comes in several forms such as nasal spray, transdermal patch, injectable, and others."

"Okay," Jim replied. "And I'm guessing we're going to Galveston because of this fentanyl. Is it somehow tied to the black-market sale of prescription medications?"

"Yes and no," Gene told him. "It's more the production and distribution of both the pill form of fentanyl and a powder form."

"That sounds like a DEA problem," Jim responded. "If there's some company or individuals making prescription medications, or any drug issue, why aren't they on top of it?"

"They're trying," Gene answered. "Most of the product coming across our southern border is from China or produced in Mexico. But it's usually the Border Patrol that's involved when the Mexican cartels bring it into the US."

"What about pharmaceutical companies?" Jim asked. "If it's a common pain relief medicine, is there potentially an issue with it being smuggled out of the factories?"

"Possibly, to a very small degree," Gene answered. "But we're looking at thousands of pounds coming across our border. It would be tough to sneak that much out of any pharmaceutical factory setting."

"What's the major issue with this drug, compared to, say, cocaine or heroin?" Jim asked as Marie came toward them with a pitcher of tea.

"Refills?" she asked, putting her hand on Jim's shoulder.

"Please," he answered as she stood looking at him for several seconds before she poured his tea.

"And you, Gene?" she asked, glancing at him.

"Yes, ma'am," Gene answered, looking from her to Jim and back.

After refilling his glass, she looked pointedly at Jim and said, "Your meals will be out shortly. Is there anything else I can do? More bread or butter?"

"I think we're good for now," Jim answered. "But thanks for asking."

Marie smiled at Gene and said, "If you decide you need anything, just let me know."

As she turned to go, she again put her hand on Jim's shoulder and smiled at him, saying, "I'll be back as soon as Dad gets the lasagna out of the oven. Your shrimp scampi is almost ready, also. Shouldn't be more than another minute or two."

When Jim looked across the table, Gene was leaning forward with his hands steepled and a not-so-subtle smile.

"I'm not going to say anything," Gene finally said, shaking his head. "Other than to say you'd be an idiot to at least not pursue this. Not to be giving you fatherly advice, but don't be an idiot."

Chapter Eight

"Now, back to the reason for the trip to Galveston," Gene continued as Marie disappeared. "You mentioned the DEA's responsibility. You are correct. It is their responsibility. In the last eight months, they've made three raids on the facility where we're sure the fentanyl is being produced."

"Maybe they have the wrong facility?" Jim asked. "Maybe they've zeroed in on a decoy that's been misleading their people."

"The possibility of that is rather remote," Gene countered. "They've had people watching the place for over a year, and they're positive it's where the product is actually being produced."

Jim sat quietly for a couple of seconds and then said, "I'm going to guess the DEA has a leak. If the production is taking place in the facility, as you say, they are positive about it. And there've been three raids, and nothing has been found; it's the only logical answer."

"That's the conclusion we've come to as well," Gene agreed, nodding. "The other part of our tasking is to uncover that person or persons and ensure their removal. But that's not the purpose of our trip to Galveston."

Before Jim could ask what the real purpose was, Marie rounded the corner with a tray and stopped at their table. Setting the lasagna in front of Gene, she said, "I hope this meets your approval, sir. Just be careful of the plate; it's very hot."

Placing the shrimp scampi on the table for Jim, she continued, "Please let me know what you think of the scampi. It's one of my favorite dishes."

"Looks great," Jim said, looking up at her. "I'm sure it will be just perfect."

Holding the tray she had carried their plates on in her right hand, she put her left hand on Jim's shoulder again and said, "Well, you guys enjoy your meals, and let me know if you need anything."

As she left, Jim looked across the table at Gene and mouthed, "Don't say a word. Not a single word."

Gene just smiled, shaking his head, and sliced off a piece of his lasagna, saying, "Finally, the obvious has been recognized. About time."

Jim twirled some pasta with his fork and speared a shrimp, saying, "Let's get back to Galveston. What am I supposed to be looking for?"

"For now, just a broad overview," Gene answered. "I've read all of the reports, seen photos or videos of everything, and been briefed by both the DEA and a couple of our people that went down last month. I just want to see for myself what we may be up against. And I want your input on how you'd handle things."

"By handling things, are we talking about removal of the people, shutting down the operation, or providing the

DEA with a clear path to their next raid?" Jim asked, taking another shrimp from his plate.

"One, all, or none of the above," Gene answered, picking up his glass. "The main purpose is to decide what approach we should take. I prefer letting the DEA do their job, and it would probably be the most efficient way to handle it. Mainly because it would mean the least exposure for Black Water."

"If your goal is to have DEA involved, why don't you spend your resources uncovering the mole in their organization?" Jim asked as Marie returned.

"Need anything, gentlemen?" she asked again, putting her hand on Jim's shoulder.

"Not for me," Gene answered, smiling. "And, the lasagna is more than *just fine,* as my young friend so ineptly previously remarked. It is absolutely fabulous. I can't say best in the Metroplex because I haven't experienced that. But it's as good as I've ever had, and I've been around the world just slightly fewer times than the moon. My compliments to the chef."

"I'll tell Dad," she said with a slight nod before looking at Jim. "And the scampi?"

"Best in the Metroplex," Jim answered, smiling at her. "I was going to say it was just fine, but I was afraid you'd whack me in the head."

"I'll tell Dad you said it was *just fine* anyway," Marie replied, smiling as she put her hands on her hips. "I'll let him come whack you in the head. He wants to meet you anyway because I mentioned your previous description of the lasagna."

"He's probably too busy to bother with me," Jim told her as he leaned back and looked up at her. "I'd hate to interrupt whatever he's working on just to come whack me in the head."

Marie looked at the empty room and replied, "I'm pretty sure he's not too busy right now since you two and another couple of tables that have already been served are the only people here. No, he has time. And being Italian, he's got to *whack* someone at least once a year. Family tradition, you know."

"Well then, if I'm going to be whacked, can you at least wait until I finish eating?" Jim told her. "I'd hate to fall face-first into the pasta and make a mess. Besides, maybe by then, there'll be some other people here, and I know he wouldn't whack me in front of witnesses."

"We'll see," she said, turning away. "I'll leave it up to Dad. But don't think you're going to get off that easy. He takes insults to his dishes seriously. I know for a fact he's had more than one food critic taken care of."

Chapter Nine

"What's Bracer's take on the mole issue?" Jim asked, reaching for his tea.

"She's got a crew monitoring every phone we've identified as belonging to any of the DEA agents involved," Gene answered. "And they're compiling a list of phones of everyone we've identified as working at the factory."

"What's the cover for the factory?" Jim asked.

"Galveston Gulf Coast Oyster Company," Gene answered. "And they process tons of oysters, in the shell by the sack or just the oyster meat in cans or jars."

"How's the financial aspect?" Jim asked, taking another shrimp from his plate.

"Looks pretty much like the other oyster production facilities along the Gulf Coast," Gene told him, blowing across the fork of lasagna.

"Same for the company officers?" Jim asked. "Maybe some middle management that's living beyond their salaries?"

"Squeaky clean," Gene admitted, shaking his head. "We've had the best forensic accountants available going over every piece of paper, bank account, asset, debt, everything."

"Then they're either the shittiest drug distribution company I've ever heard of, or you're missing something," Jim countered.

"I've come to the same conclusion," Gene admitted. "But I'll be damned if we've had any luck figuring it out. That's one of the reasons I'm going down there. And why I want your analytical expertise. Maybe I've been too close to the mistakes to see the obvious."

"Where does the company get the oysters they process?" Jim asked, trying to see a different approach.

"They get them from several suppliers," Gene answered. "Several commercial farmers around Louisiana, especially where the Mississippi River enters the Gulf, seem to be the main suppliers."

"Have you looked at them?" Jim asked. "Maybe your Gulf Coast company is buying nonexistent oysters to show the expense."

"We looked at that possibility. We ran the tonnage purchased and the tonnage put on the market, and it's in line with the other oyster companies," Gene explained, taking another roll from the basket.

"And I assume the financials of the oyster suppliers have been analyzed," Jim added, twirling pasta on his fork.

"As much as we can tell, they're clean," Gene answered. "But you have to understand that there are about 750 million pounds of oysters entering the market annually. And about 500 million come from the Gulf of Mexico."

"Isn't there something about some bacteria during the summer months?" Jim asked.

"Yes, it's called Vibrio Vulnificus," Gene explained. "Normally found during the months between April and October."

"That would limit the season to six months, then," Jim said. "Are there other sources of oysters?"

"Maine and other cold-water areas," Gene answered. "But as I mentioned, that's only about one-third of the production."

"Has the FDA been involved in looking at Gulf Coast Oyster?" Jim asked. "Maybe shutting them down because of the bacteria during those months? See if the financials change according to the drop in volume?"

"They've looked into the issue, but the incidence of illness or the occasional death is extremely low," Gene explained. "There are one and a half billion servings of raw oysters annually and only 30 reports of illness or 15 deaths. And those who died usually had some pre-existing condition, such as liver disease."

"Sounds like destroying an entire industry wouldn't be taken too kindly," Jim agreed as they saw Marie coming toward their table with her dad in tow.

"Not to mention the impact of all of the towns that rely on the oyster trade," Gene said, putting his fork down and wiping his hands on his napkin.

Chapter Ten

"Jim, Gene, I'd like to introduce my father and the Chef, Anthony Costanza," Marie announced as they arrived.

"Please, keep your seats," Tony said, motioning them to remain seated. "And make it, Tony."

Jim rose and extended his hand, saying, "Very nice to meet you, sir."

"Ah, you'd be Jim," Tony said, shaking his hand. "I remember you coming in a week or so ago. Marie has told me that you think the lasagna is, how did she say you put it, *Just Fine?*"

Shaking his head, Jim smiled slightly and explained, "I was trying to …"

"No need for any explanation," Tony said, laughing and gripping Jim's hand in both of his. "Your return says more than any words."

Turning to Gene, he laughed, saying, "And you, sir. You must be Jim's friend Gene. From the empty plate, you must have found the lasagna to be *Just Fine* as well."

"I'll confess to being this crude gentleman's friend," Gene said, standing and shaking Tony's hand. "But, as for the lasagna, I believe your lovely daughter Marie said it aptly. Best in the Metroplex.”

“It’s a pleasure to have you come dine with us,” Tony said, putting his arm around Marie’s shoulders. “But please. Sit. And with your permission, I’ll join you for a small glass of wine.”

Turning to Marie, he continued, “Marie, would you be so kind as to bring a bottle of Merlot from the reserve collection and three glasses for these gentlemen and me.”

“Of course, Papa,” she said, turning to leave.

“Now, Marie says you were a Marine,” Tony said, looking at Jim as he sat to his right.

“Yes, sir,” Jim answered, taking his seat.

“And you?” Tony asked, looking at Gene.

“Marine,” Gene said, nodding. “Matter of fact, that’s how I met Jim. We were both in Vietnam at the time.”

Turning back to Jim, Tony said, “And now Marie tells me you are a pilot for American Airlines. That must be quite a change from the Marines.”

“I can definitely say the food is better, and a hotel certainly beats a sleeping bag on the jungle floor,” Jim answered, nodding.

“Gene, are you also a pilot for American?” Tony asked, turning to him.

“No, sir. I’m afraid I’m just a little too long in the tooth for them,” Gene answered. “I quit flying when I left the Marines.”

“Except for the company jet,” Jim added. “Gene prefers the plush seats at the rear of the plane now.”

“What company do you work for?” Tony asked, looking at Gene.

"A small security company known as Black Water," Gene answered. "I'm just what you might call an advisor for them when they are negotiating a contract."

"That sounds interesting," Tony said as Marie arrived with their glasses and the wine.

"It can be," Gene admitted as Marie poured the wine and set a glass in front of each of them.

"Well, here's to interesting work and good friends," Tony said, raising his glass.

"Agreed," Jim said, raising his.

"Especially good friends," Gene added, raising his glass and nodding to both of them.

"That I can see," Tony said after setting his glass back on the table. "How long have you two been friends?"

"Over twenty years," Jim answered, looking at Gene. "A very long time."

"Do you have any children?" Tony asked Gene as Marie turned to leave.

"No, I'm afraid not," Gene told him. "You see, my wife and I always had white carpet, so it was impossible."

"You should have traded it for brown carpet," Tony replied, smiling, watching Marie leave. "Children and grandchildren are the greatest joy a man can have. Now, I must get back to the kitchen and get ready for a family who's having their reunion here in an hour or so."

"It's been a pleasure," Gene said, standing. "I'm sure Jim will be bringing me back here before too long. He seems to be quite fond of your *Just Fine* lasagna."

"Guess I'll never live that down," Jim said, standing. "It's been a pleasure meeting you, sir."

"And both of you," Tony said, shaking their hands. "Please, hurry back."

"Before you go, I have a quick question," Gene said.

"Of course," Tony replied. "What would you like to know?"

"Your surname, Costanza, is that a common name?" Gene asked.

"Reasonably so," Tony answered. "At least in Sicily. In particular among Sicilians with families going back generations. Why do you ask?"

"I'm sure you've seen the TV series Seinfeld," Gene explained. "There's a character named Costanza, George to be exact. And there's a reference to some family that's still in Sicily. I was just wondering if Costanza was a real or made-up name."

"As you can tell by my name, it's definitely real," Tony replied. "A lot of the old Sicilian families' surnames are from the professions or the providence where the family lived. So, the more generations, the more common the name.

And yes, I've seen the series," Tony smiled and continued. "I'm just hoping that particular branch of the Costanzas stays in New York."

"I guess that the Godfather, Vito Corleone, would be an accurate portrayal of someone from Sicily also," Jim mused.

"Yes," Tony agreed. "But there are many similar surnames here in the US. Take, for example, Farmer, Miller for a man who operates a grain mill, Barber, Cooper for a man who makes barrels, or Fisher. There are probably many denoting where the man is from, such as York. But now I must really get back to work. Please take your time and enjoy the rest of the wine."

Chapter Eleven

As Tony left, Marie came in and refilled their glasses with the wine, asking, "Is there anything else you guys need?"

"Not that I can think of," Gene answered. "Please tell your father thanks for the wine. That was very nice of him."

"I will," she said as she took Gene's empty plate. "Ya'll just take as long as you like. It'll be about an hour or so before the party that will need to be seated back here arrives.

And if you would like another bottle of wine, it's on the house," she continued taking Jim's plate.

"That's not necessary," Gene told her. "But thanks anyway. I need to drive back to Love Field shortly, and I've had quite enough, along with the beer we had before we came here."

"Very well," she said, putting her hand on Jim's shoulder. "I'll be back in a few minutes to check on you."

"Back to the Galveston issue," Jim said, watching Marie walk away, "Has anyone looked into the companies that do business with the Oyster Company?"

"Some, what do you have in mind?" Gene asked.

"You guys seemed to have delved pretty deep into every facet of the Oyster Company," Jim answered. "And some into the companies that supply them. But you haven't said if you've looked into their customers."

"Not really," Gene admitted. "Just a look at the volume coming in compared to what they ship out. Do you think that's where the connection is?"

"Possibly," Jim answered, taking a sip of his wine. "Hell, it could even be one more step removed from the Oyster Company. Maybe it's another layer further removed to insulate the parent company."

"I'll have the folks back at Quantico get on it," Gene said, nodding. "I'm positive that we know about the production, but with a probable leak in the DEA, maybe we can sneak in the back door unobserved and work backward."

"Worth looking into," Jim said. "I bet the computer nerds can scour their financials without much time or effort. Maybe see a thread tying some of the personnel from different organizations together."

"I'm grasping at straws right now," Gene told him, nodding. "Any other possibility is better than what we have now."

"What's the value of the fentanyl?" Jim asked.

"Street value, in the order of two hundred dollars for a gram," Gene answered. "Price varies somewhat, but I'd say a hundred fifty to two hundred."

"So that would be a little over five thousand dollars for an ounce," Jim mused. "Hell, that's close to ninety thousand dollars per pound."

"Pretty lucrative," Gene agreed. "It doesn't take a rocket scientist to see why it's a growth industry."

"What's a normal, let's call it dosage?" Jim asked.

"Probably around a milligram," Gene answered. "Anything over two milligrams is potentially lethal."

"A thousandth of a gram," Jim said, shaking his head. "Hell, that's only pennies for a dose. You'd have to have thousands of users."

"There are probably hundreds of thousands," Gene informed him. "It's also added to coke, heroin, methamphetamines, and others to induce a more intense high. Some people don't even know they've taken fentanyl until it's too late."

"I'm guessing that would make fentanyl deaths pretty high," Jim said.

"About 150 daily," Gene said. "And it's particularly high in the eighteen to forty-five-year-olds."

"That's over fifty-six thousand per year," Jim added as Marie came into the room. "I don't know what percent of users die from it, but if it's one out of a thousand, that means over fifty million users."

"Now you understand how lucrative the business is," Gene told him as he took his credit card out of his pocket.

"Anything else, gentlemen?" Marie asked as she got to their table.

"Just our check, please," Gene answered, handing her his credit card.

"Not this time," Marie said, smiling, pushing his hand away. "Dad said this evening's meal is on him."

"That's too kind," Gene told her. "But please … "

"No," Marie said firmly while smiling. "Maybe next time we'll charge you double."

"That works for me," Gene said, putting his card back in his pocket. "Especially since it'll be Jim's turn to buy."

"I'll take us to Whataburger tomorrow," Jim said, laughing. "Then we'll come back here to make it Gene's turn again."

"I just hope you come back soon," Marie said, looking at Jim. "Dad makes a lobster dish that I think you'll really like."

"I don't remember seeing any lobster dish on the menu," Jim told her.

"It's not on the menu," Marie answered. "But if you'll let me know when you're coming back, I'll make sure to have Dad make it for you."

"Only if you'll have it with me," Jim told her as they stood. "I certainly wouldn't want to have a special meal cooked for me and not have someone to enjoy it with."

"I'll talk to the Chef and see if he can do without me for an hour or so," Marie replied. "I think I can talk him into giving me a little time off."

"And I guess I'm not invited," Gene said, shaking his head. "I get treated to a burger, and Jim gets lobster without me. Now my feelings are hurt."

"You're invited, also," Marie said as they headed for the door. "Any friend of Jim's is always welcome. Even for a special off-the-menu meal."

"I appreciate that," Gene replied. "But it's much easier for Jim to pop in for a *special meal* since he lives here. I, on the other hand, have to travel a thousand miles to get here."

"Just so you know, you're always welcome," Marie told him. "No matter how far you have to come."

"Thank you," Gene said as they approached the exit. "And I'll make sure Jim brings me back here next time I'm in town. And thank your father again for his hospitality."

Turning to Jim, Marie said, "I hope you'll be back soon since you don't have to go a thousand miles to get here."

"I will," Jim said as Marie took his arm. "And I'll give you a call tomorrow about going out for drinks if you're still interested."

"More than ever," she said, standing on her toes and kissing his cheek. "I'm looking forward to it."

Gene looked at his watch and said, "Marie, it's been a pleasure, but I have a plane to catch. Hopefully, we'll get a chance to talk again soon."

"I guess that means I've got to go with him since he brought me," Jim said, blushing slightly from her kiss. "Thank your dad again for me, and I'll talk to you tomorrow."

"Guess that about removes any doubt about it," Gene whispered as they walked to his car. "You're going on that date. But we need to go get your pickup, and I'll meet you at Love Field."

Chapter Twelve

"What did you say Marie's husband's first name was?" Gene asked after they had taken off from Love Field.

"David," Jim answered. "Why do you ask?"

"We, Black Water, may be able to assist in identifying the person responsible for his shooting," Gene told him.

"There have been some dramatic changes in the technology we've developed in facial recognition," he continued as he picked up the phone from beside his seat.

"Bracer, Gene here," he said, holding up a finger. "What's on your radar these days?

Get someone else to look into that," he continued after a slight pause. "I've got a couple of higher-priority issues I want you to concentrate on.

First, let's dig into the companies that are on the receiving end of the Oyster Company's production," he ordered. "I want to know as much detail about their operations, personnel, and financials as we did with the Oyster Company."

Pausing for a second and looking at Jim, he then said, "Next, have someone look into the shooting of a police officer named David Thompson down in Dallas a couple of years ago."

Listening to her request for more information, he replied, "That's all I know. But there can't be too many Dallas police officers named Thompson who were shot on duty in the last century. So, go with that.

I'm sure you can get the cooperation of the Dallas police department," Gene continued. "Have one of the folks from Domestic Law Operations contact them and ask for any information regarding the shooting.

Apparently, there was some video footage that wasn't clear enough for a positive identification of the shooter," Gene told her. "Let's run it through the new version of our facial recognition program and see what pops up."

Again, listening for a minute, he continued, "No, it doesn't have to be a hundred percent positive. Just find anyone with over a, let's say, eighty percent match and then find out their locations within two days of the event."

Shaking his head, Gene said, "No, this is not to be released to the Dallas police. This will be strictly an internal operation and limited in access to you and whoever you have do the research.

And as far as the researcher goes, it's just an operational test of the system resulting from a change in the programming," Gene added.

Seconds later, he said, "The first priority is the oyster companies or sales outlets we've discussed. I'd like to have as much as you can get on those companies as quickly as you can. Jim is with me, and we'll be looking into the Galveston operation early tomorrow if you can get me the information before we leave the hotel."

Nodding, he disconnected the call and immediately placed another one. "Martin, Gene here," he said, glancing out the window. "Have you sent the FDA credentials and paperwork for our inspection of the Galveston Gulf Coast Oyster Company for tomorrow morning to our hotel in Galveston?"

Pausing for the answer, he then continued, "Good. And I'm sure you haven't mentioned this to anyone.

Now, as soon as we hang up, I want you to place a call to their headquarters telling them that an FDA inspection of their facility will take place tomorrow morning," Gene directed. "Identify Raymond Bolls and Anthony North as the inspectors.

No, just tell them it's a routine health code inspection," Gene added. "But before you make the call, notify Bracer's group to monitor the list for possible DEA communications. She'll know what it's for."

As Gene replaced the phone, Jim asked, "Why are you having the company look into David's shooting if you're not going to pass any information on to the Dallas police?"

"First, the technology we're using hasn't been approved for identification within the judicial system," Gene answered, leaning back in his seat.

"It'll take some time before it can be used as evidence within the legal system," he continued. "But, I'd say it's a thousand times more accurate than the current facial recognition technology.

Now, that renders the information pretty much useless as far as bringing the shooter to justice," he clarified. "At least as far as the law is concerned. But we, as you know, don't always have to stay within the strict guidelines of our legal system."

"If you do determine who the shooter was," Jim asked after thinking for a second, "What do you plan on doing with the information?"

"We can discuss that if and when we get the results of the search," Gene answered. "But, I'm pretty sure you'd be very interested in knowing who made your friend Marie a widow."

Chapter Thirteen

The following morning Gene and Jim met in the dining room at the hotel for breakfast. As the waiter left after taking their order, Gene asked, "Did you get a chance to go over the data regarding the customers of the Oyster Company?"

"A little," Jim answered as he poured coffee from the carafe. "Nothing really jumped out, but I did notice that some of the companies that purchase oysters from them seem to have a set order. That is to say that there's not much variance in the orders throughout the year."

"That's not really that abnormal," Gene replied, pouring his coffee. "Lots of companies contract for a set amount of product on an annual basis. Matter of fact, sometimes they pay a penalty unless they do. Provides both parties with stability for financial forecasting."

"I can see that," Jim agreed, nodding. "I'd like to get more information about the sales of those companies, especially those that are pure retail, to see if there may be the same trend. I don't think the ultimate user, the restaurant, can predict consumption that accurately.

And to compound the problem, oysters have such a short shelf life," he continued as the waiter approached. "I would expect their orders would vary substantially from month to month or even week to week."

"That's true," Gene agreed as the waiter put his Spanish omelet on the table. "And since that depends on whether or not they are shucked and how well the refrigeration is, it can be as short as two or three days.

They can be frozen," he continued as the waiter set a small bowl of pico de gallo on the table. "That extends the life but ruins the flavor that most people associate with fresh raw oysters."

"How long can they be kept frozen?" Jim asked as the waiter put his Western omelet in front of him.

"Maybe six months," Gene answered, spooning the pico de gallo over his omelet. "But most restaurants won't do that because of the lack of flavor. As a rule, I'd say that if raw oysters aren't eaten within two days, the restaurant will toss them out."

"And then there's the chance of someone eating a spoiled one," Jim added as the waiter put a bowl of Picante sauce and another of sour cream on the table. "Unfortunately, I've experienced that issue a couple of times. Not very pleasant."

"So have I," Gene agreed, cutting a chunk of his omelet off. "I think I went through a pound of Imodium A-D before I got control of the problem. But, I'm still a fan of chilled raw oysters."

"Me too," Jim agreed, pouring the Picante over his omelet and spooning the sour cream across the top. "Guess that's just one of the risks one takes. I wish there was a foolproof way to avoid eating one besides taste, but once the oyster touches your tongue, it's too late."

"Back to the subject," Gene said, taking another bite of his omelet. "I agree that there's probably more volatility in the retail side of the market, but I'm sure that's built into their supply forecast and with the knowledge that a certain amount will spoil and need to be tossed."

"I guess the same is true as any restaurant," Jim agreed. "Everything has a shelf life. Lettuce, basil leaves, tomatoes. The restaurant has to factor spoilage into their ordering along with trying not to run out of a high-demand item."

"I'll have Quantico get us a further breakdown of the entire wholesale and retail chain," Gene said as he took the last bite. "Just be prepared for some mind-numbing number crunching. There could be hundreds of companies dealing with the Oyster Company. Even thousands."

"What else do I have to do for the next couple of days?" Jim asked, finishing his breakfast. "I don't really expect to find much with our *inspection* today. So, I'll at least have something to look at for the next couple of days."

"Speaking of the next couple of days," Gene said as he signaled for their check, "Have you picked a day to go take Marie out?"

"Yea," Jim answered, taking a final sip of coffee. "I'll go back tomorrow afternoon. I just need to get to Love Field by two o'clock so I can get to the house and change clothes."

"What are your plans?" Gene asked after handing the waiter a credit card. "Just drinks? A game of pool at the VFW?"

"No, we're going to the Texas Roadhouse," Jim answered, standing. "They've got a pretty good steak menu, and we can have a couple of drinks before we order."

"That sounds better than just going out for drinks," Gene agreed as they headed for the exit. "More time together. Now, do you plan on coming back down here afterward, or do you anticipate a longer evening with Marie?"

"I see where you're headed with that," Jim replied, smiling. "But this is going to be just dinner. I plan on going home … alone. And I'll be ready to come back the following morning whenever you want me back here."

"I'll get back to you on that," Gene said as they got to his car. "Much of that depends on what Black Water comes up with on our requests and also what we find, or don't find, today and tomorrow morning."

Chapter Fourteen

As they pulled into the parking lot of the Oyster Company, the first thing they noticed getting out of the car was the briny smell.

"Is that the ocean or the oysters?" Jim asked as they headed for the building with the *Galveston Gulf Coast Oyster Company* written in italics across the front of a large white brick building.

"Probably both," Gene answered as they followed the crushed shell pathway to what appeared to be the entrance, even though there were other sets of doors on the side of the building with paths leading to the parking lot.

"Good morning, gentlemen," a petite dark-haired lady said, greeting them from behind a slightly raised desk with two computer screens and a telephone with numerous lines. "How can I be of assistance?"

Gene stepped up to her desk and handed her a letter with the FDA emblazoned across the letterhead, saying, "I'm Doctor Raymond Bolls with the FDA, and this is Doctor Anthony North, my associate."

Showing her their credentials, Gene continued, "You should have received notification of our inspection a couple of days ago that laid out our areas of interest and the request for the company's assistance."

"Yes sir," she replied, looking at the letter. "Our CEO, Colonel Jason Strong, informed me and told me to make sure you were given the utmost assistance on anything you need. I'll inform him that you are here, and I'm sure he'll be right out.

There are drinks just to your right in the waiting area," she informed them as she picked up her phone. "Please help yourselves while I get Colonel Strong on the phone."

Ignoring the stainless steel coffee urn and the mini-fridge with drinks, Gene and Jim walked around looking at the various pictures of oyster boats, scenes of workers carrying sacks of oysters, and what appeared to be the assembly line from years ago.

Set against a side wall, a very large tank held several oysters of varying sizes, as well as a few small fish. As they were looking at the tank, a tall, slender man in a grey suit came walking out of the doors behind the receptionist and approached them with a smile, saying, "Gentlemen, I'm Jason Strong. CEO of the Galveston Gulf Coast Oyster Company, and I'm here to assist you in your inspection. What can I do to help get this started?"

Both Gene and Jim turned from the tank and showed him their FDA credentials, and Gene said, "I'm Raymond, and this is Anthony. I'm happy to see that the company is ready to provide full support and would like to start with what I'd like to call the standard visitors' tour."

"Of course," Jason agreed as he pointed toward the doors he had come through. "If you follow me, we'll go to our delivery area, and you can follow an oyster from the sack it arrives in to where it ultimately leaves to find its way to the plate of some lucky patron at one of the numerous restaurants we serve across this vast country of ours."

Leading them down a long hall with closed doors every several feet, he continued, "This is our administrative section where orders are taken, bills sent out, responses to requests such as yours are processed, and our labs where we are continuously monitoring the cleanliness and sanitation of every square foot of the company."

Approaching the end of the hall, he continued, "When I say every square foot, that's exactly what I mean. Since any of our numerous people who work here may be required to visit the actual working floor, we make sure any microbe or bacterial residue they may have picked up on their shoes doesn't contaminate our facility."

Turning right in another long hallway covered with windows on one side, Jason motioned to the area behind the windows and told them, "As you can see as we walk along, there are a hundred people working in this section. This is where we determine which oysters are destined to be raw in the shell or processed into jars of just the meat of the oyster."

As they approached the end of the hall, he told them, "When we enter this section, you'll see conveyer belts bringing the oysters from the unloading docks where we accept shipments to our first sanitation station. Before we enter, we'll be putting disposable rubber boots over our shoes, and it will cover the bottom of our pants. This is to prevent transferring any foreign material from this section to the next."

Entering the massive room, they watched as a long conveyor belt was loaded by hand as workers wearing white coveralls with white hoods and goggles emptied sacks on the wide rubber belt and spread them across its width, trying to ensure no two oysters were touching.

"This is the first step," Jason told them as they watched the workers who occasionally tossed an oyster into a barrel beside his workstation. "Any oyster that doesn't look right or is open, indicating it is dead, is tossed into the rejection barrel."

Watching it slowly travel into the interior of the production area, it passed beneath several sprayers; he discussed the pressure and temperature of the water along with the chemicals used to wash the shell as they passed beneath them, as well as the UV-C light that was designed to kill any bacteria on the shells.

Just past the sprayers, a group of workers dressed the same were reexamining the oysters and turning them over for the next rinse station. Again, some oysters were removed from the line.

"How many employees do you have?" Gene asked as they followed the moving belt.

"Usually about a thousand," Jason answered. "What you see here is just one shift. Due to the nature of the product, we have to be able to operate around the clock. Twenty-four hours a day, three hundred and sixty-five days a year."

"That's quite a feat in itself," Jim added, nodding. "To keep that many people on staff all year long must be difficult."

"It is," Jason agreed. "That's why I offer excellent pay and benefits. As well as having one of the best HR departments in the business. It's always difficult to attract and keep good employees, but it's especially difficult in this business.

As you can see already, it's a rather repetitive process, but without the attention paid to each and every oyster, the wrong one could get past us and cause insurmountable problems for our company," he finished as they watched the belt pass through an opening in the wall. "Now, we'll go to the next section where decisions must be made as to where the individual oyster goes."

Chapter Fifteen

"As I told you before, this is where we determine if the oyster is to be shipped raw in its shell or processed into just the meat," Jason said as they entered a small area with a shelf of booties and a barrel. "But you'll need to exchange your soiled booties for new ones.

The people you see here beside the incoming belt are making that decision with only a second's look at the oyster," he told them as they entered. "As you can see, the majority remain on the belt and will ultimately be shipped in their shells.

The other belt where they are placing oysters will go to the canning process where the shell will be opened and the meat extracted to be placed in jars," he said as the workers' hands flew across the belt, picking oysters from the first belt and placing them on an adjacent one that originated at their location.

"I noticed that even here, there are rejections," Jim mused, watching one of the workers toss an oyster into a barrel beside her.

"And you'll continue to see that," Jason assured him. "Even more so when we get to the canning area. Once the oyster is opened, it becomes even more evident that something may render that particular oyster unusable."

"Can we see that process first?" Gene asked. "Then we'd like to return and follow the raw oysters to the end of their journey."

"Certainly," Jason answered, leading them to another door. "We'll be replacing the booties again before we go into the next section."

"Hell, the cost of these booties must be considerable," Gene mused as he pulled the new booties over his shoes.

"Not really," Jason said, replacing his. "Not too many people pass through each section in any one day. Most come to their section and never leave until their shift is over."

"What about breaks?" Jim asked.

"Their break rooms are within their section," Jason answered as they entered the next section. "They aren't required to change booties unless they use the bathroom facilities. Then they must replace them before stepping back onto the production floor."

As they entered, the first thing they noticed was that all of the workers were sitting at stainless steel tables with a barrel beside them. Using a rake to drag the oysters from the slow-moving belts, they then deftly popped open the shell and put the meat in the tub with a layer of ice and the shell on a conveyor belt running above the belt that brought the oysters in.

"Once the tubs are full, about twenty pounds, a worker will come get it and take it into the next section," Jason informed them as they watched men bringing in fresh tubs and taking the full ones from the room. "As you can see, the belt bringing the oysters in splits into three separate belts that travel to the workstations. That allows the belts to travel at one-third of the speed of the one bringing the oysters in.

That's about how long these people have to open the oyster, make a decision, and not have a slowdown that would ripple throughout the production."

"Who has the authority to shut down the line?" Jim asked, watching the speed at which the lady in front of him was removing the oyster from its shell.

"There are three supervisors in this section, and any one of them can do it," Jason answered. "In the first two sections, there's only one since they don't require as much manual labor as this one."

"Anyone else?" Gene asked.

"Of course," Jason said, turning to look at him. "Any of our lab personnel can stop the entire process down if they determine there's a problem with bacteria or microbial issues.

Matter of fact, they have the authority to not only shut down the facility, but they can also have every single oyster that's been on the line removed as contaminated," he finished. "That includes even those that have completed the process."

"That's got to be a real problem," Jim said, thinking about how many oysters that would involve.

"That's why we take samples every fifteen minutes," Jason told them. "That way, we know which section was contaminated, and the time to go from one section to another is always twenty minutes. If we detect any problem, it's isolated quickly, and we don't lose the entire production line."

"That's smart thinking," Gene told him, nodding. "Now, could we go see the section that produces the raw oysters?"

"Certainly," Jason answered, heading for the exit. "Will you be taking a lunch break after that?"

"If you have other duties, we'll do so," Gene said as they left the section. "We'll do everything we can not to disrupt your operations."

"That would be great," Jason said as they entered the next section. "I have a staff meeting scheduled and would like to take care of that before we see what else you need to inspect."

Chapter Sixteen

After watching the raw oysters being inspected once again before being placed in sacks, Gene told Jason that they'd be back in an hour or so and followed him through the exit, where they tossed their booties.

As they left the building, Gene asked, "What do you think?"

"Denny's," Jim answered. "I'm sort of ready for a chicken fried steak with mashed potatoes and gravy."

"I was more interested in what you thought about their operation than what you wanted for lunch," Gene said as they reached their car.

"I figured so," Jim said, opening his door. "But I thought I'd save you the time of asking me where I wanted to eat and then answer your real question as we drive."

"Okay, Denny's," Gene said, backing the car from the parking spot. "Now, the other question?"

"I honestly didn't see any place they could be running a drug production," Jim answered, shaking his head. "At least nothing we've seen so far would lend itself to producing a powder or tablet. The entire environment is too moist for something like that.

And I didn't see anyone that would look like they worked in a lab," he finished.

"I agree," Gene said as he headed south on Rosenberg Street. "Maybe it's inside the admin part of the building. Maybe the lab is actually making the fentanyl as well as checking for microbes."

"Possible," Jim agreed. "I don't know how much space or time would be involved in the fentanyl production, but I guess they could do it while waiting for their mandatory inspection every fifteen minutes."

"That does seem to be a limiting factor," Gene agreed, turning east on Seawall Blvd. "Guess we'll have to take a look at the lab and the number of people working there. I'm also going to have Quantico get me some infrared photos of the facility to see if there's possibly any area that isn't being used today.

Then, we can compare that with the areas we've been escorted through," he finished as they pulled into the parking lot at Denny's.

"That would be a big help," Jim said, getting out of the car. "That place is sort of linear, but there could be areas between the production floor and the rest of the building that might house their other activities."

As they were being led to their table, Gene pulled his phone from his pocket and answered, "Barker."

"Iced tea, unsweet," he quietly told the waiter as he listened to his phone.

"Fine, send it to the hotel," he said. "And have someone get me some infrared photos of the Oyster Company within the next hour and have them delivered to my room. I'll swing by and get everything when we finish lunch.

Well, a little good news for you," Gene said as the waiter was returning with their drinks. "I'll tell you later, but I think you'll be happy."

"Are you gentlemen ready to order?" the waiter asked, setting their drinks on the table and looking at Gene.

"I'll have the country-fried steak with mashed potatoes and fried squash," Gene answered, taking a sip of his tea.

"And you, sir?" he asked Jim.

"Same," Jim answered. "And could you please bring a bottle of Tabasco?"

"Of course, sir," the waiter said, scribbling on his pad. "I'll be back with your orders as soon as possible."

Waiting until the waiter was out of hearing range, Jim asked, "What's going to make me happy?"

"We think, that is what Black Water thinks, we have identified the shooter from Marie's husband's death," Gene answered.

"That was fast," Jim observed. "The Dallas police department had gone over every piece of evidence for over a year and came up with nothing. How did Quantico get an identification in less than a day?"

"They sort of have a new facial recognition program," Gene answered. "Something your old friend Bracer developed."

"How does she find more than what I'm assuming is state of the art can do?" Jim asked. "There's only so much that can be done with a picture, depending on the pixels and all sorts of other things. Distance from the camera. Camera focal length. Amount of light. Stuff like that."

"I don't have a clue about how it actually works," Gene admitted. "But I do know it's something to do with a computer taking the images from David's body camera, the dash camera from his car, and the reflection from within the car.

Then, they somehow use the images from the suspect's rearview mirror, his side mirror, and, as I said, the reflection off the windshield and side windows," he continued. "Then the computer takes all of these images and comes up with a face that they then try to match to their massive file of practically everyone in the world's face.

We'll get into it a little more after lunch," Gene concluded as the waiter brought their meals.

Chapter Seventeen

After eating, they headed for the hotel before returning to the Oyster Company, and Jim asked, "So who did they come up with?"

"Man named Jack Robertson," Gene answered as they drove west on Seawall Blvd. "They're running background checks on him now. I should know more by tomorrow."

"Is there some connection between him and David?" Jim asked as they turned north on 61st Street.

"Not that they told me," Gene answered as they approached the bridge on Offatts Bayou. "But, they've only now made the identification.

The thing you have to remember is that it took a lot of computer time to piece together all of the images," he continued, turning left on Broadway. "Then they took all of the possible matches and did a search to see which ones could have possibly been in Dallas on the day David was shot."

Pulling into the Galveston Inn and Suites, he said, "Once they had eliminated all but Jack Robertson, they then did a quick search of his criminal record. Some drug use and suspicion of distribution."

"So, do they think it was just a random chance that he picked David?" Jim asked as they walked up to the front desk.

"Not sure," Gene answered as he waited for the clerk to come to them. "Let's give it a day or two before we try to figure out what his motive was. It's possible it was something personal between him and David.

Do you have any packages for either Bolls or North?" Gene asked as the desk clerk arrived.

"Just a moment, sir," he replied as he looked beneath the counter.

"Yes, sir," he said, placing two large envelopes on the counter. "These just arrived a few moments ago."

"Thanks," Gene responded, taking the envelopes and turning toward the elevators.

Once in Gene's room, he handed Jim an envelope saying, "Here are the infrared photos. See if you can see anything that might be a possible lab area that we didn't see when we were there."

Gene looked at the data regarding the companies that purchased the Oyster Company's products. Seeing dozens of companies that received weekly supplies of raw oysters, he did a quick check to see if there were any noticeable differences in the quantity each received.

Not seeing anything that might raise suspicions, he then looked at the single company receiving just the meat. The company, Bayou Canning, was the only one, and their volume was fairly constant.

"See anything?" Jim asked as he held a photo up for Gene to see.

"Looks like a large facility with a lot of heat spots throughout," Gene responded. "What are you seeing?"

Jim pointed to a section that appeared to be an extension of the production line, saying, "All of the other areas show activity. This area shows none. Yet, it's clearly part of where the oysters are processed."

"And you think that may be where the lab is located?" Gene asked, looking at the photo again.

"I don't know," Jim responded, shaking his head. "I think it's a little too large for just a lab and as I said, I don't really know how much space a lab that makes fentanyl needs to be. But it needs to be checked out when we go back."

"Agreed," Gene said, handing Jim the papers he had been looking at. "Take a look at these as we head back, and tell me if anything stands out."

Jim left the photos on the table in front of the couch and stood as he accepted the papers from Gene. "How much more time do you plan on spending at the Oyster Company?"

"Not a lot," Gene answered as they left his room. "Probably a couple of hours to finish the tour. Did you have anything specific in mind?"

"No," Jim told him as they left the elevator. "I was just thinking about what we need to do tomorrow if we finish the tour today."

"I don't know if we need to do anything tomorrow if we finish today," Gene told him as they got in the car. "Are you thinking about going back home this evening?"

"No, tomorrow about noon is still good with me," Jim answered as they left the parking lot. "I was thinking about if there was another oyster production facility around that we might get a quick look at to see if there are any major differences."

"That sounds like a good idea," Gene said, pulling out his phone. "I'll have Quantico do a quick check and set something up if there is."

Chapter Eighteen

As they entered the lobby of the Oyster Company, the receptionist picked up her phone as she watched them approach.

"Colonel Strong will be right out," she told them. "Is there anything I can help you with while you're waiting?"

"No, ma'am," Gene replied. "I can't think of anything."

"I do have a question," Jim said.

"Hopefully, I can answer it," she said, smiling.

"Did Colonel Strong serve in the military? And if so, which branch?" Jim asked.

"I'm afraid I don't know the answer to that," she answered, shaking her head. "I just know that he's been Colonel since I came to work here."

"How long have you worked here?" Jim asked.

"Almost three years," she answered as Jason came through the doors. "I'm working on a degree in marine biology at the Galveston Community College. I've become very interested in it since coming to work here."

"Gentlemen, how was your lunch?" Jason asked as he reached them.

"Fine," Gene answered as they stepped from the desk. "Now, if you wouldn't mind, we'd like to follow the raw oyster line."

"No problem," Jason said, leading them down the hall again. "Anything in particular you're interested in?"

"How much of your production is in the raw end?" Jim asked as they entered the hall that ran parallel to the production line.

"Usually about eighty to ninety percent by volume," Jason answered as they entered the line area and pulled on their booties.

"Is that pretty much in line with other producers?" Jim asked as they approached where the belt feeding that area entered.

"I'd say so," Jason answered as they watched the conveyer belt covered with oysters move. "As far as our operation, there's at least three times as much manual labor getting the meat out of the shell and out of the door. So, the real profit is in the raw oyster."

"Who do you primarily sell the shucked oyster to?" Gene asked, watching workers filling sacks at the end of the belt.

"Bayou Canning," Jason told him. "They are our sole customer. And they are also a part of the overall corporate structure.

Actually, they were the initial company my grandfather started," he continued. "They only got into the production end when my father took over the company and saw where the raw oyster portion could be developed."

"Not to be nosy," Jim said. "But which branch of the service were you in?"

"You're, of course, referring to my title of Colonel," Jason answered, smiling. "I'm afraid it's purely ceremonial.

My great-great-grandfather was in charge of a small group of militia in Louisiana during the Civil War," he continued. "One of the conditions he demanded before he would accept surrender was that he, and all of his male descendants, would be awarded the honoree title of Colonel when they turn twenty-one.

So, the answer to your question is I have never been in any branch of the service," he concluded. "Now, we'll follow the sacks to their resting area before being transported to the buyer."

"We didn't see where the shucked oysters went after the tubs were picked up," Gene offered as they left the area. "Where did they go?"

"They went into a cold storage area where the tubs are combined until ready for shipment to the canning company," Jason answered. "We usually ship at the end of the day, and the canning takes place during the night."

"I thought you said you operated here twenty-four hours a day," Jim observed as they headed back down the hall.

"I believe I said we had the capacity to operate twenty-four hours a day," Jason corrected him. "Normally, we have two shifts of eight hours. We can call in a third shift if necessary. Or we can have the evening shift stay overtime."

Opening the door to the area where the sacks were being stored, Jason continued, "I'll show you how we can expand the operation to a full three shifts as soon as we leave here if you'd like."

"That'd be great," Gene said as they watched the sacks being put into a large walk-in cooler.

"How long do the oysters remain in the cooler?" Jim asked, looking inside.

"Usually, they are shipped out the following morning," Jason answered. "You've probably noticed that we keep the entire production line slightly cooler than you might expect. Here, the oysters are kept at fifty degrees until the distributor picks them up.

His trailer is also refrigerated to fifty degrees," Jason said, turning to look at them. "The same is true of the shucked oysters. Except that they are kept on ice until delivered to the cannery. And *cannery* is a misnomer since we put our oysters in glass containers of varying sizes depending on the volume the customer wants.

Now, would you like to see the area where we can expand our operations?" he asked, turning from the cooler.

Chapter Nineteen

As they entered the next area, both Gene and Jim looked at each other, realizing that this was the area they had wondered about.

"If we get overloaded during either shift, we can call in additional help, and the raw lines will continue into this area," Jason explained. "We don't use this area for shucking the oysters due to the increased possibility of bacterial spread if we're trying to run both operations here."

"So, this isn't for the third shift?" Gene asked as they looked at the empty room and motionless conveyor belts.

"No," Jason emphasized. "It's purely to increase the raw oyster production. It's rare, but sometimes we get overwhelmed with the volume, especially during the fall through winter months.

I'm sure you've heard the old adage about not eating oysters unless the month has an *R*, haven't you?" Jason continued. "Well, when the production from the oyster beds in the gulf cranks up, that's added to the production from the oyster farms.

The farms provide us with about two-thirds of our raw material," he explained. "So, we have a somewhat stable product line coming in since they can control their beds more than Mother Nature does. Thus, when there's a bounty from the gulf beds, we can ramp up to take advantage of the increase."

"That sounds good," Gene told him, turning to Jim and asking, "Is there anything else you'd like to see before we leave?"

"I'd like to see the lab and take a look at their findings for the last three months," Jim said, looking at Jason. "And I'd like to see the temperature logs for each section for the same period."

"That's not a problem," Jason said as he turned to exit the area. "If you'll just follow me, I'll introduce you to the chief of our laboratory and let him provide you with any information you may need.

Is there anything else you need from me?" he asked as they entered the hall leading back to the administrative part of the building.

"I don't think so," Gene told him. "I appreciate your help, and hopefully, everything else will go as smoothly as this has been."

"I appreciate your help also," Jim added. "It's been informative and educational. I didn't realize how labor-intensive the oyster business was. I guess it'll be a while until a machine is invented that can take the place of a human."

"I wish there was a robot that could shuck the oysters," Jason said as they approached a door marked *Laboratory*. "That would save most of my labor costs. The only other invention I wish someone would come up with is something that could spot a bad oyster without having to open it. But until then ..."

Opening the door into the lab, Jason motioned for a short, bald man with a white lab coat to come over. As he arrived, Jason said, "Randy, these gentlemen are from the Food and Drug Administration, and they have a few questions regarding your area of expertise."

After introducing them, Jason turned to look at Gene and said, "If you decide you have any further questions or desires, please just let my receptionist know, and she'll find me."

"Thanks again," Gene said. "I'll try not to bother you again, and unless there's some major issue with the lab, I'll close our inspection and notify headquarters that no discrepancies were discovered."

"That'd be great," Jason said, heading for the exit. "I don't believe you'll find a better-run facility in the country."

"Now, gentlemen," Randy said as Jason left. "How can I be of assistance?"

"I'd like to see your bacterial reports for the last three months," Jim answered. "And I'd like to get a copy of your inspection procedures checklist and follow you through your next line inspection."

"While you're with Anthony, I'd like to see the last three months' temperature readings," Gene told him. "I'm hoping we can get out of your hair in the next half hour."

"You shouldn't have much problem getting out of my hair," Randy said, smiling. "There isn't much left. But I'll have one of my assistants take care of you since the next line inspection is due in three minutes, and I'll do it myself."

Randy took a copy of the inspection checklist and handed it to Jim, saying, "I'll get you the reports you asked for when we get back, but it's imperative that we maintain strict adherence to our inspection schedule, as I'm sure you can understand."

"Completely," Jim said, following Randy out of the room.

Chapter Twenty

As Jim and Randy returned to the lab, Gene was placing a stack of papers on one of the nearby lab tables. "How'd it go?" he asked, turning to Jim.

"We'll see shortly," Jim answered. "As soon as Randy can run the swabs and see if there're any bacteria, I guess I have no further itcms to look at."

"I finished looking at the temperature data, and there are no deviations worth discussing," Gene replied as he watched Randy using a microscope to examine each sample he had taken.

"All clean," Randy said, looking up. "Would either of you gentlemen care to look and verify my findings?"

"I don't believe that's necessary," Gene answered, getting a headshake from Jim. "I believe we've taken enough of your time, Randy. Thanks for your cooperation, and we'll note no discrepancies in your lab procedures in our report."

Looking at Jim, he continued, "Well, if you've nothing to add, we need to get back to the hotel and finish our report."

"I'm ready," Jim said, nodding to Randy. "I was going to see if there was a restaurant near the hotel that served raw oysters for dinner tonight … but I think I've seen and smelled enough oysters for the next few weeks."

"I understand," Randy agreed, leading them to the exit. "After all the years I've spent handling them and even knowing that they are generally safe to eat raw, I, too, spend enough time around them. I'll take a good steak, baked potato, and Caesar salad."

Passing through the reception area, Gene thanked the receptionist for her help and told her to thank Jason for his assistance.

"What now?" Jim asked as they approached his car.

"We see if Quantico has found us another facility to visit," Gene said, unlocking the doors to the black Suburban.

"I still don't think I saw any place in the entire facility where I'd suspect to find a lab that's producing what I'd consider a very dangerous drug," Jim said as they left the Oyster Company.

" If fentanyl is produced as a powder, it has to remain dry," he continued. "The entire facility is extremely damp, therefore unsuitable. And, depending on how absorbent it is on the skin, I just don't think the filtration systems would protect the workers in any area we visited."

"What are you saying?" Gene asked as they headed west on Seawall Blvd. "You think Black Water is wrong about the Oyster Company being involved in the fentanyl trade?"

"I didn't say that," Jim countered, shaking his head. "I just don't think they are in the production end. I can see them on the distribution side. But I don't think Black Water is correct in its conclusions.

Maybe that's why the DEA never found anything," Jim continued. "They're looking in the wrong area. Hell, there may not even be a mole at the DEA."

"So, what do you think our next move should be?" Gene asked as they neared their hotel.

"Not sure," Jim answered. "But I'd like to look at whichever oyster facility we get a chance to visit. Especially if it's today while everything is still fresh in my mind."

"I'll call my office as soon as we get back to our rooms," Gene said, turning onto Broadway. "Maybe we'll get lucky."

Chapter Twenty-One

Shortly after arriving back at the hotel, Gene called Jim's room and told him to meet him in the lobby in ten minutes to head to San Leon where they were expected within the hour.

"What's happening at San Leon?" Jim asked as he stepped from the elevator to find Gene waiting in the lobby.

"Quantico arranged for an unannounced inspection of a small oyster wholesale company there," Gene answered, heading for the parking lot. "We'll be using the same names and credentials as before. I hope you brought yours."

"It's still in my pocket," Jim answered as they got into the car. "What's this place called?"

"It's the Fresh Bay Oyster Company," Gene answered as he drove east on Harborside Drive. "I don't have much information on them other than they process oysters for wholesale much as the other Oyster Company does."

"Is it close to the same size?" Jim asked as they merged with the light traffic heading north on I-45.

"Probably half as big an operation," Gene replied as they crossed the bridge onto Tiki Island.

"They'll be closing for the night in about two hours," he continued past Bayou Vista on another bridge. "So, what area do you want to concentrate on?"

"I guess sort of the same thing we did before," Jim answered. "Start with the arrival of the oysters and follow them to the end. We should be able to do that in less than an hour."

"Let's do this," Gene suggested as they passed through La Marque on I 45, "I'll look at the lab and check their inspection and temperature logs while you follow the oysters."

"Sounds good to me," Jim said, nodding.

A few minutes later, pulling into the parking lot for the Fresh Bay Oyster Company, Jim said, "I don't think this place is even a quarter the size of the other. The buildings are much smaller."

"Yes, they are," Gene said, getting out of the car. "Maybe they only process twenty-five percent as many oysters."

"We need to get those numbers," Jim told him as they approached what appeared to be the administration building. "That way, we can compare the two."

"Agreed," Gene said, opening the door. "I'll have Quantico do an aerial photo run and get an IR scan as they do it. And they can do a quick financial analysis to see how much product they sell."

"Good afternoon, gentlemen," the lady receptionist said as they approached her desk. "How may I help you?"

"I'm Doctor Raymond Bolls, and this is Doctor Anthony North," Gene answered as they both presented their FDA credentials. "We've just been directed to make a quick inspection of your facility, and I believe headquarters sent notification of our arrival either late this morning or early this afternoon."

"Yes, Mr. Jerry Nelson, my boss, just informed me minutes ago to expect you," she replied. "I'll let him know you're here."

As she replaced her phone, she told them, "He's on his way. It shouldn't take more than a couple of minutes. Is there anything else I can do for you while you're waiting? There are coffee and soft drinks behind you in the waiting area."

"We're fine," Gene responded, looking around at the small area as a door behind the receptionist opened.

"Gentlemen," a tall white-haired man said, walking toward them. "I'm Jerry, and it'll be my pleasure to assist you in any way possible."

"Good afternoon, Jerry," Gene said, shaking his hand. "I'm Raymond, and my associate here is Anthony.

I'm terribly sorry for this short notice inspection, but we finished another inspection earlier than we thought it would take," Gene apologized. "We'll try to make this as quick and painless as possible and make sure we're out of your hair by your normal closing time."

"Whatever you guys need, we'll make time to accommodate you," Jerry said, shaking Jim's hand. "Where would you like to start?"

"I'll be looking at the lab," Gene answered. "Anthony will be looking at your processing area."

"No problem," Jerry said, turning to lead them through the door he had come in. "I'll take you to our lab director, Doctor Paul Bunyan, and yes, that's his name. I told him to expect you right after I received the request from the FDA office.

Then I'll take Anthony to our production line," he finished as he opened the door to the lab.

As they entered the lab, two men in white lab coats came over, and the older man introduced himself as Paul and his assistant Rob.

"Paul, this is Doctor Bolls," Jerry said as the men shook hands. "If you'd provide him with anything he requests, I'd appreciate it."

"Just call me Raymond," Gene said as he shook hands.

"If you guys will excuse us," Jerry told them, "I'll take Doctor North to the line and let him see our operation."

Chapter Twenty-Two

Less than an hour later, Gene and Jim thanked Jerry for his assistance and promised him a favorable report before leaving the building.

"So, what do you think?" Gene asked as they left the parking lot.

"Pretty much the same operation as before," Jim answered. "But, if I remember correctly, the first Oyster Company said they sent eighty or ninety percent out as raw oysters."

"That sounds familiar," Gene agreed as he joined Farm Road 646 heading north.

"This one says they're closer to seventy percent raw and thirty percent shucked," Jim told him. "And another thing I noticed was how they handle the shells after extracting the oyster from the shell."

"How was it different?" Gene asked, merging onto I-45 and going south.

"The first one placed the shells on a conveyor belt running toward the unused area," Jim answered. "This one tossed them into barrels, and a forklift carried them out of the processing line."

"Why do you think that's important?" Gene asked.

"I asked Jerry what happened to the shells, and he said they are carried outside and left to dry," Jim answered. "Then, they are crushed or bagged and left for about six months in the sun to kill any bacteria. The bagged shells are then used to help promote additional oyster growth by building a sort of manmade reef of shells.

Or, sometimes, the crushed shells are used in concrete or anything else that needs a high calcium content," Jim continued.

"Okay, but what do you think happens to the shells from the Oyster Company?" Gene asked as they retraced their route back to the hotel.

"I'm not sure," Jim answered. "But they seem to be interested in keeping the two halves together on the conveyor belt, whereas the last one just tossed the shells in the barrels."

"I still don't get where you're headed with this," Gene said as they crossed the bridge back onto Galveston Island.

"I'm not sure myself," Jim admitted. "But it seems strange that there's a discrepancy in the percent raw oysters processed and the method of handling the empty shells."

"The ratio of raw to shucked could be due to different marketing," Gene said as they pulled into the hotel parking lot. "As to the handling of the shells, maybe it's because of the volume. Adjusted for volume, maybe it's closer to the same number of oysters shucked."

"I'd like to see what the Oyster Company does with the shells," Jim said as they headed for the hotel. "Jerry showed me the pile of shells outside the building where they were waiting to be picked up by some other company that actually recycles the shells.

I'd like to see if there's a pile of shells outside the facility at the Oyster Company," Jim continued. "Is there any way we can get a return visit to check it out?"

"I don't think so," Gene told him as they approached the elevators. "It might raise suspicions. But I'll have Quantico get some high resolution photos that should confirm if they are piling the shells the same as Jerry does."

"I guess that'll have to do," Jim agreed. "Have them photo Jerry's place also, and that way, we can make a comparison."

"I'll make the call when I get to my room," Gene said as the elevator doors closed. "Now, when do you want to go back to Dallas, and where would you like to eat tonight?"

"Noon tomorrow is good for going home, and I was going to say steak, but that's what I'm having with Marie tomorrow evening," Jim answered as the elevator rose. "How about seafood since we're close to the source?"

"Sounds good to me," Gene told him as they got off the elevator. "I believe I saw a seafood restaurant just down the road. "I'll notify Black Water to make sure the plane's ready tomorrow, and I'll meet you in the lobby in thirty minutes."

"Sounds good," Jim replied as he opened the door to his room. "I just need a quick shower to get this stinking oyster smell off and some clean clothes on."

Chapter Twenty-Three

As Jim stepped off the elevator, he spotted Gene talking on his phone in the lobby. When he joined him, he heard Gene saying, "Great. Send them to me. Jim and I will look it over."

"Good news, I guess," Jim said as Gene put his phone in his pockct.

"Indeed," Gene answered, nodding. "I'll give you a quick update on the way to the restaurant. Ready to go?"

"Definitely," Jim told him as they left the hotel.

"That was the folks at Quantico," Gene said as they got in the car. "They've traced every shipment of oysters to twenty-seven different distribution centers across the country. And they're delving into the owners, shareholders, or anyone with ties to each of the companies."

"Isn't that normal for a company as large as the Oyster Company?" Jim asked as they left the hotel parking lot.

"That I don't know," Gene told him as he turned onto Broadway. "But one small piece of information they discovered was who owned twelve of the twenty-seven companies.

It seems that those companies are located in some of the largest cities in the US," he continued, turning south on 37th street.

"That doesn't seem abnormal," Jim countered. "I'd even say that it would be logical to have distribution centers in the largest population centers possible."

"Agreed," Gene explained. "But these twelve companies are all owned by different private corporations."

"I'd think that's normal, too," Jim argued. "Unless they're some chain such as Lowes or Kentucky Fried Chicken with franchises, I don't see any red flags."

"It's in the board of directors at these corporations that's the key," Gene told him as they turned left on Avenue S. "The CEO of each one is the same man."

"So, we've got the same man on the boards of these corporations," Jim mused. "That's certainly not normal."

"Definitely not," Gene agreed, turning left on Seawall Blvd. "And an even more interesting thing is that none of the other board members appear to be real."

"Fictitious people along with identical CEOs," Jim remarked as they saw *BLVD Seafood* ahead on the left. "Are there any direct ties with the Oyster Company?"

"Other than all of them being customers, not that we've discovered," Gene answered, pulling into the parking lot. "But they're doing a deep dive into the backgrounds of the CEO and Jason or any of the other upper-level people associated with the company."

"I can see a slight possibility that the CEO may have set up those twelve corporations for tax purposes," Jim said as they headed for the restaurant. "Or for liability reasons. But why use fictitious people? Why not a Limited Liability Corporation, an LLC?"

"I agree," Gene replied, opening the door for Jim. "There are several legitimate ways to have the same tax and liability protections without such subterfuge."

"Good evening, gentlemen," the hostess said as they approached her podium. "How many?"

"Just the two of us," Gene answered, smiling.

Picking up two menus, she said, "If you'll just follow me, I can seat you immediately."

Once seated, Gene said, "Before I forget it, the plane will be ready to take you home at eight o'clock tomorrow morning."

"What are you going to do here while I'm gone?" Jim asked, looking at his menu.

"I'm going back to Quantico after we drop you off at Love Field," Gene answered, setting his menu down. "I don't think there's any reason to stay here any longer since it appears that you were right about the conditions not being conducive for a fentanyl production facility as we thought."

"What do you plan on telling Black Water?" Jim asked as their waiter approached with a tray and two glasses of water balanced on his right hand.

"That we were wrong," Gene answered as the waiter set their glasses on the table.

"Good evening, gentlemen," the waiter announced. "I'm Marty, and I'll be taking care of you this evening. Would you care for cocktails before dinner?"

Gene took a quick look at Jim and answered, "A very dry vodka martini sounds good to me. Grey Goose if you have it. Shaken, not stirred."

"Of course, sir," Marty said with a slight bow. "And for you, sir?"

"The same except with a cocktail onion," Jim told him.

"Excellent," the waiter said. "I'll be right back with your drinks."

As he left, Jim asked, "What's our next move? And do you think Black Water is going to pass on the contract since there's little evidence that they can assist the DEA?"

"Let me ask you this," Gene replied, leaning forward and putting his elbows on the table. "Do you think they should? Or do you think there's something there? Probably not the production, but in the distribution?"

Jim leaned back and took a moment to think about his answer and finally said, "Something's fishy, and I'm not talking about the oysters. Now, knowing that their distribution channels are suspect, I'm even more convinced that they're involved. I just don't know exactly how."

"I agree," Gene said as their drinks arrived. "Now I just have to convince my boss that it's still a viable contract, but we'll need a little more time to tie the ends together."

Setting their drinks in front of them, Marty asked, "Are you ready to order, or do you need a little more time?"

"I believe we're ready," Gene answered, picking up his menu and handing it to Marty. "I'd like the shrimp and grits."

"Excellent," Marty said, writing on his pad and turning to Jim asking, "And for you, sir?"

"The Texas shrimp," Jim said, handing his menu to Marty. "Grilled, please."

Chapter Twenty-Four

The following morning, Gene was having coffee in the lobby when Jim stepped off the elevator. Walking to the complimentary coffee bar, he selected a cup of regular black and a blueberry muffin.

Taking a seat across a small table from Gene, Jim asked, "Is the plane ready?"

"Whenever we get there," Gene answered, finally looking up from some papers he was reviewing. "You ready to go?"

"Anytime," Jim answered taking a bite of the muffin.

"Finish your muffin, and we'll head out," Gene told him, passing a couple of photographs across the table. "While you're eating, take a look at these."

Jim picked the photos up and studied them for a few seconds and then said, "Looks like Jerry's oyster production has a pile of oyster shells almost twice as large as our Oyster Company."

"Using whatever magic the photo folks have, Jerry's pile is 2.3 times as large," Gene confirmed. "Now, the only thing we don't know is how long Jerry has been adding to his pile and how long ago the Oyster Company had their shells hauled away."

"So, this information is useless," Jim mused, tossing the pictures back on the table.

"Not really," Gene argued. "It's a baseline. We'll make another photo run in a couple of days and compare the results. And then we'll have some data to compare to the number of oysters each company brings in."

"I wish I'd had this information when we were there yesterday," Jim remarked, sipping his coffee. "At least I would have had a few more questions to ask."

"And I wish I knew why the chicken crossed the road," Gene said, smiling. "But I don't. All I know is which side of the road he's on now, and I have to deal with the information I have."

"Point taken," Jim agreed, nodding. "Anything new on the CEO and his fictitious board of directors?"

"Yes," Gene answered. "Not only is one man, whose name happens to be Michael Gilliad, the CEO of the twelve companies, he's also the CEO of four other companies. And one of these four is the parent company of the other three."

"Let me guess," Jim remarked, shaking his head, "The other three companies are parent companies of the original twelve."

"You are wise, grasshopper," Gene said, gathering the papers and photographs. "That is exactly what's happening. And, for the final step, at least that we've discovered so far, Michael and Jason are both on the board of yet another company known as *Yellow Brick Road*."

"And Yellow Brick Road is the parent company of all of the other companies," Jim surmised.

"Correct, sir," Gene replied. "And the CEO of Yellow Brick is Jason's wife, Maria."

"All this is very interesting," Jim said, finishing his muffin. "But does it put us any closer to figuring out the Oyster Company's role in the fentanyl issue?"

"No, but it's further evidence they're involved in something they're trying to keep from the public," Gene answered, standing up. "Just more fodder to use to make my case that we should continue looking into the operation. It's just gotten more widespread now."

"Anything else on the companies that supply the Oyster Company?" Jim asked as he tossed his empty coffee cup into the trash.

"Not much," Gene told him, heading for the exit. "Every supplier seems legit so far. Do you have any thoughts on that?"

"Not yet. Just keep digging. If the Oyster Company is just a distribution center, they have to be getting the fentanyl from somewhere," Jim admitted, following Gene to the car. "I think we need to solve the distribution issues first. Hell, we don't even know if there is something illegal happening. It could be as simple as tax dodging. Or a way to conceal income from an unhappy divorce."

"By the way, take a look at this as I take us to the airport," Gene said, handing Jim a manila envelope as they arrived at the car. "We can discuss it as we fly back to Love."

Chapter Twenty-Five

As they headed north to Love Field, Gene was on the phone with Black Water as Jim sat reading the material Gene had handed him as they left the hotel.

When Gene finally ended his last call, Jim asked, "Is Black Water completely sure Jack Robertson is the man who shot David?"

"Absolutely," Gene assured him, nodding. "Since the original identification, Bracer's bunch of nerds has been monitoring him through his phone. Not only do we have the photographic evidence, but we also have a recording of him talking about taking out a cop.

During that conversation, he describes where and when he made the hit," Gene continued.

"Did he give any reason why it was David?" Jim asked. "Was it personal?"

"They haven't heard if it was or not," Gene answered. "He was just bragging about shooting him. Mr. Robertson is a pretty nasty customer and not a very bright one at that.

As you already know, he's been arrested several times involving drug use and suspicions of distribution," Gene continued. "He also has some loose connections to a couple of the Aryan Nation groups. Current speculation is that the hit was to gain points with one of them."

"Why would shooting David gain points for him with the Aryan Nation?" Jim asked.

"Our research shows that David's grandmother was Cherokee," Gene explained. "She was married to one of the men who participated in the land rush in Oklahoma in 1889. The pictures of him show a definite Native American heritage background.

There's also the possibility that Jack had a run-in with David somewhere in the past that didn't get recorded, and he held a grudge against a *non-Aryan*," Gene finished.

"Tell me again why we can't just turn this over to the Dallas Police and let them take care of Jack Robertson," Jim said, looking at the pictures once again.

"And just how would we be able to explain that?" Gene answered. "We're using technology that doesn't exist in the civilian world. And we used some fairly intrusive measures without any warrant or consent from Robertson.

If it were to go before any judge in even Texas, it would be tossed," Gene explained. "I doubt any District Attorney would even attempt to get an indictment."

"Then what do you expect me to do?" Jim asked, already knowing the answer.

"What do you want to do? That's what's at issue," Gene told him. "I'm not advocating any action whatsoever. But we, the company, just want you to know who shot Marie's husband. What you do with the information is up to you."

"How much support can I expect from the company if I do decide to take some action?" Jim asked as he rolled the idea around in his head.

"I'm sure you'd receive absolute support," Gene told him. "That I can guarantee."

"How soon can you get me a deep search into his habits, the groups he's been wooing, and his known associates?" Jim asked.

"Probably within forty-eight hours," Gene answered. "Especially since I've had Bracer on it for a day or so."

"Pretty sure of my reactions, aren't you?" Jim said, setting the material on the small table beside him.

"Pretty sure," Gene replied. "The only thing I have any doubts about is how things will be between you and Marie after your date tonight.

But I'm pretty sure that by the time we can get the data you're going to need, you'll already have a plan in mind," Gene finished.

"Not that I'm that far into my thinking," Jim said, looking at Gene, "But how much of this fentanyl does it take to kill someone?"

"Probably two milligrams," Gene answered.

"Is it possible to acquire a few milligrams surreptitiously?" Jim asked.

"I'm sure that can be arranged," Gene told him, nodding. "We have our sources."

"And we know that Jack has an addiction problem?" Jim asked as a plan began to form.

"Maybe not exactly an addiction problem, but he's no stranger to using," Gene answered.

"I'd be interested in how much, how often, from who, what type, and any other information about his daily routine as possible," Jim told him. "But, if I do decide to take some action, it's not because of Marie. It's just that allowing anyone to shoot a policeman and walk away is contrary to my moral code."

"I know," Gene said, smiling. "And I know that sometimes a reason for taking an action can be accentuated by how close a relationship is to someone who was harmed. And knowing you as I do, the closer the relationship, the more reason to exact revenge."

Chapter Twenty-Six

As soon as the plane dropped him off, Jim headed home in his pickup, still thinking about the issue with Jack. He had to admit it to himself, but not to Gene, that his desire to remove the man was more because of Marie than because he shot a policeman.

Once home, he tossed his suitcase in the bedroom and decided to wash the Corvette before cleaning up for his date. Trying to decide if he was doing that just to impress her or whether he should just drive the truck, he had a thought about the supply issue.

Knowing that Gene was still flying to Quantico, he dialed his number and waited for it to be answered.

"I have a thought," Jim said as soon as he heard Gene's voice.

"Well, that's something new," Gene remarked. "Does it make your head hurt?"

"No, but something is definitely a pain in my butt," Jim retorted. "Now, would you care to hear it, or would you rather swap insults?"

"Go ahead," Gene said. "I'm listening."

"We know that the Oyster Company is using all of the other companies to obfuscate their activities," Jim started. "Now, if you were involved in the distribution end, you'd need a secure source on the supply end.

If it was me, I'd make damn sure I had control of that," Jim continued. "I bet that if you search their suppliers, you'll find either Jason's or that Gilliad guy's name somewhere in one of them, if not more."

"That is a good idea," Gene acknowledged. "I'll make a call right now. Oh, are you taking the 'Vette on your date or that nasty ass pickup?"

"Well, I thought about taking the 'Vette, but I want her to be impressed with me instead of my car," Jim answered.

"Take the 'Vette," Gene told him. "You're not that impressive, and you need every advantage you can get."

"Thanks, General," Jim said, laughing. "Let me know what you find on that other issue. You know … the one that we're supposed to be worried about instead of my love life."

"Just take the 'Vette," Gene suggested again. "I'll give you a call in the morning and bring you up to date on what we find. Have a good evening."

Smiling, he went into the garage and rolled the 'Vette out onto the driveway. Seeing that it was just a little dusty, he pulled the hose from beside the house, did a quick rinse job, and then used a towel to wipe it down.

Seeing that he still had plenty of time, he pushed the car back into the garage and did the same for his pickup. *'Nasty ass pickup?'* he thought as he dried it. *'A perfectly fine machine if you ask me.'*

After showering and shaving, he took a quick look at Marie's address and how to get from there to the Texas Roadhouse. If there was one thing he didn't want to do, it was not to appear to know where he was going once he picked her up.

Finally dressed, he headed north on 635 and soon came to the exit for Garland Avenue. Following it north to East Avenue D, he turned right and soon came to North 1st Street. A few blocks later, he made a right turn onto East Walnut. After a right turn on Country Club Road, he soon came to Riverchase Drive. Almost immediately after turning left, he came to Myrtle Beach Drive and spotted her house.

Parking on the street abeam the sidewalk, he killed the engine and sat for a moment looking at the house. Finally getting out, he walked up to the front door and rang the bell, now glad that he had driven the 'Vette. This was too nice a neighborhood for his *nasty ass pickup.*

"Hey, Jim," Marie said, answering the door. "Please come in. I'll just grab my purse, and we can get going."

Looking around, Jim said, "I like your house. Very nice."

"It's not my house. I'm just staying here until mine is finished with some remodeling," Marie said, glancing around. "This was Mom's choice. Dad said he could live in a single-wide trailer and Mom told him that he'd definitely be single if he tried to make her live in one."

"I can understand," Jim said as they left the house. "I'm gone almost half of the time, and all I use of the house when I'm home could be satisfied with a single wide. Or maybe a one-bedroom house."

"Any problems finding our house?" Marie said as Jim held the car door open for her.

"Nope," Jim said as he shut her door. "I'm just wondering where the beach is?"

Laughing, Marie said, "I guess you'd have to go over to Lake Ray Hubbard to find the nearest beach. So, I'd say we're more beachfront adjacent."

"There was a Myrtle Beach Air Force Base in South Carolina," Jim said as they pulled out. "That's just like the Air Force. Build their bases on a beach while the Marines put theirs in the worst possible places. Swamps. Deserts. Places where no sane person would want to live."

Chapter Twenty-Seven

After being seated at the Texas Roadhouse, Marie ordered a frozen margarita, and Jim decided on a Ziegen Bock as they read the menu. A few minutes later, as the waiter put their drinks on the table, he asked if they were ready to order or needed a few more minutes.

"We'd like the Cactus Blossom to start," Jim answered. "The lady would like the eight-ounce Dallas Filet, medium rare. For sides, can she substitute a Caesar salad for one?"

"Absolutely," the waiter answered. "What would she like for the other side?"

"Baked potato," Jim told him. "And I'd like the ten-ounce Fort Worth Ribeye, medium rare, Caesar salad, and baked potato also."

"Excellent," the waiter said, scribbling on his pad. "I'll have your Cactus Blossom out in just a few minutes. Will there be anything else?"

Seeing Marie shake her head, Jim answered, "I believe we're good for now, thanks."

As the waiter left, Jim lifted his drink toward Marie and toasted, "To a great evening with a lovely lady."

"And to a fine gentleman," she replied with a slight nod.

After taking a sip, she set her margarita down and asked, "Do you mind if I tell you something?"

"Not at all," Jim said, setting down his beer.

"First, I think your little car is absolutely beautiful," Marie told him. "I can see why you like it …"

"But what?" Jim asked, smiling at her obvious embarrassment.

She looked around for a couple of seconds and then said, "It's not very comfortable, is it?"

"No, it's not," Jim agreed, laughing. "It's hot in the summer, cold in the winter, rides as rough as a buckboard, and you're not the first one to notice."

"Oh?" Marie said, looking into Jim's eyes. "I don't suppose that would be a woman, would it?"

"As a matter of fact, it was," Jim admitted. "My wife, Jennifer, had to ride all the way from California to Texas with me in that car."

He paused, looking at Marie, and said, "I made a promise to myself not to talk about her tonight. Tonight was to just get to know you."

"Me, too," Marie said, nodding. "But you have to admit, Jennifer is as much a part of who you are as David is to me. They are part of who we both are and dancing around the subject won't help."

"Agreed," Jim said, nodding. "I probably overthought the evening and didn't want to talk about any painful subjects."

"I learned months ago that talking about it doesn't make it any less painful," Marie told him, reaching across to take his hand. "But I think it clears the air … makes it less of a taboo during a conversation."

"I guess that I haven't had much conversation with anyone about it," Jim said, holding her hand. "Matter of fact, you're the only one other than Gene that I've spoken to about it."

"Well, if I'm going to get to know the real Jim Lashley, it's something we have to feel free to talk about," Marie told him as the waiter brought the Cactus Blossom.

As the waiter left, Jim placed his napkin across his lap and said, "I don't think a fine gentleman, as you put it, would order a dish that's impossible to eat without fingers."

Marie reached over, pulled two pieces of the battered onion out, and replied, "Then I guess you'll think I'm no lady when I dig in with my fingers."

Pulling a wedge from the bloom, Jim dipped it in the Cajun Horseradish sauce and replied, "Then let's forget the Emily Post rules for social etiquette and enjoy the evening."

"Emily Post," Marie said, laughing. "Now, there's a name I haven't heard in years. My aunt Adrina had a copy of one of her books. I think she used the book more to smack my dad in the head instead of a reference."

"Why would she smack your dad?" Jim asked as he pulled another piece of the onion bloom from the rapidly diminishing Cactus Blossom.

"He'd belch at the table," Marie answered, laughing. "Or some other heinous breach of her idea of proper table manners."

"I can just imagine a meal like that," Jim said as he saw the waiter returning with their entrees. "Mom would just close her eyes and shake her head. But I guess your family was a little more emphatic in their methods of expressing disapproval."

"Most assuredly," Marie said as her steak was set in front of her. "Especially my aunt. I think it's because she never married and, therefore, had no kids to see how a bunch of hungry children behave at the table.

Mother, on the other hand, sort of expected it, figuring it didn't matter at the family table," she continued as Jim's steak was placed on the table. "She tried to set a good example, definitely more so than Dad, but it was lost on us kids."

"Please enjoy your meals," the waiter said as he backed from the table. "If there's anything you need, please don't hesitate to let me know."

Chapter Twenty-Eight

"Where to now, Sir Jim?" Marie asked as the waiter returned with Jim's change.

"I don't care," Jim answered as he left a tip and slid his chair back. "I don't know much about what's up here in Garland. What do you suggest?"

"There's a little bar, more of a tavern, not too far from here," she answered as she stood. "But it's just beer."

"That's fine with me," Jim said, following her toward the exit. "Just don't let me get lost on the way there."

A few minutes later, she pointed ahead to the right and said, "There it is, Intrinsic Brewing."

Finding a parking spot, Jim opened her door and remarked, "Looks like it's popular."

"It is," Marie told him as they headed for the door. "Some nights more than others. Especially when they have some local musicians playing, but it's also rather small, which makes it look like there's a big crowd."

Marie led into the bar and spotted a table near the end of the room, saying, "There's an open table. Or would you rather sit at the bar?"

"Table," Jim answered, looking around. "Fewer people to overhear."

"You aren't concerned about someone overhearing us, are you?" Marie said as she took a seat.

"No, I just don't want to hear them," Jim said, smiling. "You might as well know it now. I'm not much of a crowd person."

"I figured that," Marie said, looking toward the bar. "You always want a table away from anyone when you come to the restaurant."

"I guess I get to hear enough about everyone's problems when I'm flying," Jim said as a waitress approached. "I prefer to just watch instead of listening to most of the people I run into at bars anyway, especially when they've been drinking. Avoids problems."

After the waitress left with their orders, Marie said, "David was a lot the same way. He just wanted to enjoy a quiet beer after dealing with the people he had to put up with all day."

"I'm sure he dealt with some rather unpleasant folks," Jim remarked as their beers arrived. "The Flight Attendants are usually the ones I have to deal with who have the urge to run their mouths. Lots of gossip about other Flight Attendants, bad marriages, unfaithful husbands, stuff I'd rather not get into a conversation about."

"Some people just have to share every aspect of their lives," Marie said, raising her beer to toast Jim. "Here's to privacy."

"Indeed," Jim said, raising his mug.

"But I certainly don't mean privacy between couples," Marie clarified. "If you can't be open and honest with someone, they might as well be a stranger."

"Agreed," Jim said, setting his beer on the table. "The best part of a relationship is having someone to understand you. Someone who doesn't need to tell you everything but tells you anyway."

Marie laughed, saying, "Now that's some philosophy, Mr. Lashley. I'm not sure I have a clue as to what you're saying."

"You're right," Jim said a moment later, shaking his head. "That makes about as much sense as baptizing a cat."

Beer sprayed from Marie's mouth as she laughed again, saying, "Baptize a cat? What the hell are you talking about?"

"Beats the hell out of me," Jim said, laughing at himself. "I guess I'm just trying to carry my end of the conversation. It's just too bad that I really don't have much to say."

"Oh, I bet there's a lot to say," Marie said, leaning over to Jim. "I'm just waiting for you to say it. Maybe it'll take a while, but I think it's worth waiting for."

"I hope you're not waiting for some pearls of wisdom to drop from my mouth," Jim said, taking her hands. "Maybe a little old-fashioned logic. But wisdom? You could be waiting a lifetime."

"I don't think you got where you are with just old-fashioned logic, Jim Lashley," Marie said, leaning across the table and kissing Jim's cheek. "You're an enigma wrapped in a riddle."

"Winston Churchill," Jim replied, smiling. "And the correct quote is a riddle, wrapped in a mystery, inside an enigma."

"Well, however, it goes," Marie said, squeezing Jim's hands, "I'm pretty good at riddles. And I do like mysteries."

Chapter Twenty-Nine

As Jim was rinsing the cup he had used for his morning orange juice, the coffeemaker gave a final sputter, signaling that it had completed its task of turning ground coffee beans into the magic elixir caffeine.

Carrying the steaming cup into the living room, he had barely taken his seat when the phone rang. "Good morning," he answered, taking a tentative sip to test the temperature.

"Good morning," Gene said. "Ready for some good news?"

"Good news? Sure," Jim replied. "Of course, what's good news for the tiger isn't such good news for the slow-moving gazelle."

"Then I'll just tell you, and you can decide whether it's good or not," Gene replied. "We did an extensive background check of every boat that supplied the Oyster Company. And found some very interesting data.

First, the boat we're most interested in is owned by a group of investors known as *The Ocean's Protectors*," Gene continued. "They are about four layers below the real owners, which includes some names you are already familiar with."

"Let me guess," Jim interjected. "How about Jason Strong, his wife Maria, and Michael Gilliad?"

"You can add Ricardo Guzman to your list," Gene told him. "He's the brother of Maria. Then toss in Jesus Martinez, the brother of Ricardo's wife Margarita."

"Okay, I've lost track," Jim admitted. "I understand that the convoluted list of people and companies is damning, but where does this get us?"

"It gets us a target," Gene answered. "The boat, named *Maria's Fortune*, is now under surveillance. It's currently in port, but we expect it to be heading out to sea in the next few days."

"How are you going to monitor *Maria's Fortune* when she heads back out?" Jim asked, trying to sort out the players in this game in his head.

"For now, we're just watching the docks," Gene replied. "What would you suggest?"

"Can we get a dedicated satellite to monitor the boat?" Jim asked. "I'd be interested in where she goes when she heads out to sea."

"I'll see if I can make that happen," Gene said. "I'm going out on a limb here and guessing that you suspect that to be the source of the fentanyl."

"I would bet on it," Jim told him. "We've agreed about the Oyster Company's inability to be in the production phase. Just in the distribution end."

"Agreed," Gene said. "I presented the data from our visit down in Galveston to Black Water, and they agreed to give us more time based on that assumption."

"Since we've eliminated one source of production, I don't believe an oyster boat would be able to handle it either," Jim continued. "That means if the boat is involved, which I'm convinced it is since it has obvious ties to all of the other pieces of the puzzle, it has to be in the distribution chain also."

"That's what we believe here at Black Water," Gene added. "Nothing else makes sense."

"Continuing to follow that thread, the boat must be meeting out at sea with someone who's the next link in the distribution chain," Jim replied. "I still don't think the lab would be on any boat. We know fentanyl's biggest manufacturers are either in China or Mexico.

With the Gulf of Mexico being such a large expanse of water to monitor, and if the transfer is beyond the twelve-mile territorial limit, the Coast Guard can't touch them," Jim continued. "I doubt if even our Navy would be authorized to board a ship at sea without some national interest.

That's where I'd do my business," Jim concluded. "But we still need to connect *Maria's Fortune* to whoever is the next step to the actual producer."

"That's the position of Black Water also," Gene agreed. "We believe the product is coming in through Mexico, and there has been too much money lost trying to bring it across the border from Texas to California. So, this is their preferred method of getting the fentanyl into the States."

"Good," Jim said, getting up to refill his coffee. "Did your people get any data on the oyster shell issue we discussed?"

"Not yet," Gene told him. "They're making daily runs across both facilities, but there's not much to be learned from only two days of observation. I'd like to see at least a week of data before I jump to any conclusion."

"So, when do we go back down to Galveston?" Jim asked, coming back to his chair in the living room.

"Probably not for four or five more days," Gene answered, then paused momentarily. "So, how did the date go last night? Did you make plans for another evening?"

"It went fine," Jim told him. "No, we didn't make any plans because I wasn't sure when I needed to go with you back to Galveston."

"Well, I'd say you have a window of opportunity of three, maybe four days," Gene said. "If you take the advice of an older gentleman, you should take advantage of it. Once we head back down south, and given your flying schedule, you may not have time for her for a while. And I don't think you want to wait for possibly two weeks."

"I appreciate the advice," Jim told him. "But I don't want to rush this."

"Fine," Gene said. "At least go have dinner at their restaurant before we need to get to work. Do something, even if it's wrong. Indecision is your worst enemy right now. And I'm betting the lady is waiting for you to call even as we speak."

"I'll let you know when you decide exactly when I need to go with you," Jim told him. "Until then, I'll figure out what I want to do and resolve the dreaded enemy … indecision."

Chapter Thirty

The following morning, Jim had just finished cleaning the sink and toilet in his bathroom, mopping the floor, and wiping down the shower when his phone rang.

"Hello," he said, tossing the towel he had used into the laundry basket.

"Good morning, Jim," Gene said. "How's your day going?"

"Peachy," Jim answered. "I've just finished cleaning my bathroom, and now it's on to the other two. But I'm sure you're not interested in my new career as a cleaning lady."

"No, but it is good to know that you have other interests besides the mundane life of an airline pilot and international assassin," Gene said. "But I am interested in what you have planned for the day besides cleaning your toilets."

"Well, I do need to mop the kitchen floor," Jim said, laughing. "If you'd like to help, I'm sure the other floors need some cleaning as well."

"Maybe next time," Gene replied. "Anyway, I'm going to be landing at Love Field about two o'clock this afternoon.

Do you have anything planned for the evening … I mean after you finish your housework?"

"As a matter of fact, I do," Jim answered. "Marie called me yesterday afternoon telling me her twins are coming down for a couple of days, and she's invited me to have dinner with the family this evening."

"So, meeting the family," Gene told him. "Sounds serious to me."

"Dinner," Jim replied. "Let's not get ahead of ourselves. I'm sure you remember Marie saying her dad made a lobster dish. Well, it turns out that the girls wanted Lobster Scampi tonight. So, Marie asked me if I'd like to join them."

"I guess I can take care of what I need to come down for in a couple of hours so you can enjoy the lobster," Gene said with sarcasm dripping in his voice. "I believe I saw a Whataburger between your house and the hotel where I'm staying."

"Okay," Jim said, smiling. "Don't try to pull that *poor pitiful me* crap on me. I'll call Marie and see if she can accommodate one extra person."

"Don't let me interrupt your intimate dinner," Gene said, teasing him. "I'm not one to interfere in the magic of a happy couple. But, if you insist, I'd love to join you … and the family."

"I'll make sure you're invited," Jim said, shaking his head. "Now, what are you coming down for this time? I thought you wanted to wait a few more days regarding the oyster shells."

"I'll tell you more when I get there," Gene answered. "I do have a little information on that issue, but this is more about Jack Robertson.

Mainly, we need to discuss what I believe you were hinting at when we last talked about what to do with him," Gene continued. "I'm not sure what you are thinking is the best way of resolving the issue."

"I'm open to suggestions," Jim said, nodding. "Especially since I'm depending on Black Water's support."

"Good," Gene replied, smiling to himself. "I'll see you around three this afternoon. I'll give you a call when I've checked into the hotel, and you can let me know if I'm welcome at the family dinner."

"I'm sure it's not going to be a problem," Jim said, shaking his head. "But I'll give you a map of the best burger places near Love Field if they turn down my request."

"Good," Gene said. "Now, I've got to get back to work on a couple of items before my plane leaves. And I'm sure you need to go dust something. By the way, what color apron are you wearing?"

Before he could answer, Jim knew Gene had hung up. Smiling, he called Marie to see if there had been any changes to the dinner plans.

"Good morning, Marie," he said as she answered. "How's your day going?"

"Fine," she responded. "The girls should be here in about an hour, and I'm making sure their bedrooms are ready."

"I have a request," Jim said, picking up the pair of socks he had left hanging on his boots. "My friend Gene is coming down this afternoon to discuss a few things, and I was wondering if it would be all right if he joined us for dinner this evening?"

"Certainly," Marie answered happily. "I'll let Dad know. He always makes twice as much as we can eat, but I'll make sure. Is seven o'clock still a good time? Or do we need to delay it for Gene?"

"Seven is good," Jim told her. "I'll see you then."

"Looking forward to seeing you," Marie replied. "And your friend. I'm sure the girls will enjoy meeting him as well."

Chapter Thirty-One

Jim was in the driveway washing his truck when Gene pulled to the curb in his customary black Suburban with dark tinted windows. Tossing the sponge he was using into the bucket of soapy water, Jim rinsed his hands and walked down to greet him.

"How was the flight?" Jim asked as they shook hands.

"Pretty much normal," Gene told him, looking at the soap covering the hood of the truck. "Shouldn't you wash that off before it dries?"

"Probably be best," Jim answered as they walked toward the house.

Picking up the hose, he started spraying the soapy residue from the truck and said, "Dinner's not until seven this evening. Would you like to clean up after the flight?"

"Not necessary," Gene said, watching as Jim finished. "I stopped by the hotel, took a quick shower, and changed clothes. But I think you'll need to do a little sprucing up before we go."

"No doubt," Jim replied, dumping the bucket and rinsing it out. "I figured I'd take care of that after we discuss the reason you're here and maybe have a beer."

Rolling up the hose, Jim said, "I've been thinking about what you said regarding Jack. I remember the trouble we had setting up times when we used poisons or other chemical methods. It took several people, and the timing had to be exact.

So, I've come to the conclusion that I'll follow the old school ways and go Old Testament on him," Jim said as they entered the house. "Like with those assholes, may they roast in hell and the Devil fork them daily forever, who killed Jennifer."

"I suppose you'll need our help," Gene replied, taking a seat on the couch.

"It would be appreciated," Jim told him, heading for the kitchen. "Would you like anything to drink?"

"Got any tea?" Gene answered as he put a large envelope on the coffee table in front of him.

"Just made it yesterday afternoon," Jim answered as he filled two glasses with ice.

Then, squeezing a wedge of lemon for each, he filled them from a pitcher from the refrigerator. Carrying them in, he set one in front of Gene and carried his to the recliner where he sat.

"Before we get into the Jack issue, I want to bring you up to date on the oyster shells," Gene said, taking a sip of his tea.

"First, understand that this is still preliminary, but we've managed to contact the companies that contracted with both of them to remove the shells once a week," Gene continued. "There is a remarkable difference in the ratio of shells removed and oysters delivered," he said, looking at one of the sheets of paper before handing it to Jim.

"I think you'll notice that Jerry's company averages almost fifty percent less shells than the Oyster Company," he said. "Now, that by itself could be explained by the differences in the number of raw oysters versus shucked oysters. But, if you'll remember, the Oyster Company told us they send out eighty to ninety percent as raw oysters, and Jerry said about seventy percent raw.

Doing the math, the Oyster Company is way under the amount, by weight, of what they should be disposing of according to the number of oysters they process," Gene finished.

"Then what's happening with those shells?" Jim asked as he finished reading the report.

"That's one of the things we need to look into," Gene answered. "And one other thing we've discovered is that Maria's Fortune only makes one run per week. One of our guys got to talking to some of the boat operators at one of the local bars where they go when in port and discovered that little tidbit of information."

"What's the normal?" Jim asked.

"In for two to three days, then they go back out," Gene answered. "Depends on how far they have to go to get to the reefs. There are almost twenty-three thousand acres of public reefs and just a little over two thousand private leases. So, it could make a big difference.

But, according to the people we talked to, Maria's Fortune stays out longer and nobody's seen her more than a day at any of the most lucrative areas," Gene finished.

"I guess we'll know what's happening when we get the satellite coverage," Jim mused.

"Another anomaly is that Maria's Fortune normally arrives later in the day," Gene added. "Usually after sunset. It's not a big issue, but it's just another piece of the puzzle. Add that to the fact that none of the crew seems to want to socialize with the other oystermen. Again, another piece. And the pieces are adding up to a very suspicious operation."

Chapter Thirty-Two

For the next couple of hours Jim and Gene theorized about what the different possibilities were regarding the entire operation and what areas needed to be investigated.

Finally, Jim announced that he needed to get ready to go to dinner and told Gene to make himself at home while he waited.

"Take your time," Gene said, pulling out his phone. "I've got a few calls to make to get things going regarding what we've discussed."

When Jim came back into the living room, Gene had just finished a call and remarked, "You certainly did shine up for this casual family dinner."

"Normal Wranglers and shirt," Jim replied. "Nothing I don't usually wear when I go out to eat."

"You forget that I've known you for many, many years," Gene reminded him, smiling. "I know the difference between a first-time worn since back from the cleaners pair of starched jeans and the same for the white shirt. Not to mention the extra shine on the boots."

"There's always a first time worn since *back from the cleaners*," Jim retorted, shaking his head. "Now, if you're through giving me a ration of shit, let's head over there."

"I'll bet you don't clean up like this when you go out by yourself," Gene teased as he led the way to the door.

"No, I don't," Jim agreed as they headed to Gene's car. "Sometimes I go to Whataburger in my work clothes. But this is different."

"How's it different?" Gene asked as they pulled from the curb.

"White tablecloths," Jim replied. "And clean restrooms."

"And a special lady," Gene said, smiling. "You'll never convince me that this isn't a special evening either. Especially knowing that you'll be scrutinized by her daughters."

"Does this car have a radio?" Jim asked, shaking his head. "I'd rather listen to some talk show host blather on about some inane subject than to carry on this conversation."

"It's broken," Gene said, laughing. "I'm your entertainment for the next few minutes until we get there."

"Then, can you drive any faster?" Jim said, joining in on the laughter.

After arriving at Siciliano's, they were greeted at the door by Marie's mother, who said, "Jim, welcome back. And I believe I'm correct in welcoming back your friend Gene."

"Yes, Ma'am," Gene said with a slight bow. "And first, I'd like to thank your family for allowing me to join you this evening. That's very gracious of you."

"Think nothing of it," she replied. "By the way, I'm Aurora, and it's my pleasure to meet you."

"Don't let her name fool you," Anthony said as Marie followed him from the kitchen. "Her name may mean

Roman Goddess, but I can assure you that she should have been named for the goddess of bad temper."

"You hush," Aurora said playfully, slapping his shoulder. "Otherwise, I may tell them what your name means."

"I'll tell them right now," Anthony said, leading them to the back of the restaurant. "It means worthy of praise."

"Ha!" Aurora whispered as they approached the table where places had been set for five. "If it weren't for the other diners here, I'd tell you what it really means."

"Mom, you and Dad behave yourselves," Marie told them, putting her arm across Jim's shoulders. "I wasn't planning on letting Jim know our family secrets until after the second bottle of wine."

"Ah," Anthony said as the twins came in. "Gentlemen, may I present the loves of my life, besides my lovely Aurora, of course, my wonderful grandchildren.

First, because she was first born, Giosepa," he continued. "Named after my grandfather Giuseppa and her obvious twin sister, Giulia."

"Aren't you going to tell them why you named me Giulia?" one of the girls said with a slight wave to Jim and Gene. "And I'm better known as Julie."

"And most people call me Seppa," the other daughter told them. "And Julie still thinks just because her name means youthful, she'll be eternally young."

"Younger than you," Julie said, sticking her tongue out at her sister.

"Five minutes. Big deal," Seppa responded, making a face.

"Enough about our family," Aurora announced. "Tony, you get back to the kitchen, and I'll take care of our guests. Jim, you and Gene, please take a seat. Marie, if you would please pour our guests a glass of wine. And girls, mind your manners. We aren't back at college with a bunch of addle-headed juveniles."

Chapter Thirty-Three

Marie took Jim's hand and said, "Please sit here, Jim."

As she took the seat to his left, she continued, "Gene, would you please take the chair beside me? Girls, please be seated."

"Aren't your mother and father going to join us?" Gene asked as everyone sat.

"Not until later," Marie said, pouring Gene's glass half full. "Mom will be back and forth until closing, and Dad will swing by when he gets a chance."

Just as she finished pouring her wine and Jim's, Aurora came in with three platters of Bruschetta, baskets of steaming bread, and plates of butter, saying, "Please, eat. Anthony won't start your lobster scampi until he's sure it won't overcook."

"Girls, each of you can have one glass of wine," Marie told them as she put a piece of the Bruschetta on a small plate in front of Jim. "And maybe I'll let you have a small glass of Dad's secret stash of Cognac."

For the next thirty minutes, the girls discussed their lives as college students and Jim and Gene told them about their education and time in the military. Marie was content to let her daughters carry on the conversation as her mother came in every few minutes to check on them.

When the last piece of Bruschetta wound up on Julie's plate, Aurora told them that Anthony would start their scampi. Checking to see if they might need more bread or butter, she said, "Marie, please take care of anything our guests need. I'm going to be busy for the next half hour as our other guests leave."

"Sure, Mother," Marie said, nodding. "Don't worry about us. I can take care of everything back here."

"So, Gene," Seppa started, "And I hope it's all right to call you Gene since I don't know your last name."

"It's Barker," Gene answered. "And yes, Gene is fine with me."

"Mom told us Jim works for the airlines," she continued. "What do you do since retiring from the Marines?"

"I work for a company that provides security services for companies who need it," he answered.

"Kind of like the Secret Service?" Julie asked.

"More or less," Gene told her. "But we aren't part of the government. Sometimes, we are hired by the government to do research, and sometimes by other nations' governments. But mainly, we work with private companies."

"Is that sort of like being a spy?" Seppa asked. "I mean, researching for the government into security stuff."

Gene laughed and answered, "No. I think you've been watching too many James Bond movies. We're more like a research assistant to one of your professors. Sometimes, we do hire former military members to provide security for visiting dignitaries if they don't bring their own.

But that's a very small part of our business," he explained. "No 007 stuff. However, Jim does order his martinis shaken, not stirred. That's about as close to being a secret government agent as he'll ever be. And me as well."

"Mom said you sometimes come down to have Jim help you," Seppa continued. "Does that mean he's one of the people you hire to be a security guard?"

"No," Gene told her, shaking his head. "Jim's busy enough flying airplanes for American Airlines. I sometimes come to discuss some of our possible contracts with him.

Mainly because he's had a lot of experience with security issues during his years in the Marines," he finished. And we're more like friends sitting around discussing a problem. Sort of like you guys probably do when given an assignment at college."

"You said you sometimes work with the Secret Service," Julie said. "Do you ever work with others, like the FBI?"

"Sometimes," Gene answered. "Sometimes state law enforcement, sometimes cities hire us."

"Does that mean you can help find someone?" Julie continued. "Like maybe the guy that killed our dad?"

"I'm afraid that's a little out of our expertise," Gene answered. "We just don't have the resources to do something like that. Our research is mainly looking at people's backgrounds if they're from another country seeking a security job here in the US.

Besides, anything we could do wouldn't be usable in any court," he explained. "Especially since it was so long ago."

"Well, it's like it just happened yesterday for us," Seppa joined in. "I can't believe that the police can't find at least someone who knows something. Isn't that their job?"

Chapter Thirty-Four

"So, how's everything going back here?" Anthony asked, coming in to join them.

"Excellent," Jim answered. "Except I may have eaten so much of the delicious Bruschetta that I won't have room for the lobster."

"Did you hear that?" Anthony said, looking surprised. "Those words of praise coming from the man whose best review of my most popular dish has been *just fine*. Must be the wine."

Anthony finally smiled at Jim and said, "I think you'll find room once you taste my lobster scampi."

Taking a wine glass from an adjoining table, he asked, "Marie, would you mind giving me a couple of inches of wine before I return to the hotter-than-Hades confines of my kitchen."

After finishing the wine, he continued, "I'll be back in about five minutes with the main course. So, I'd advise you to save any room you have left."

As he left, Aurora came in with a fresh pitcher of ice water and rounded the table topping off each glass.

"Aurora," Jim began as she filled the last glass, "Are you aware that there's a small town just north of Fort Worth named Aurora?"

"No," she said, pausing to think. "I've heard of one in Colorado."

"This one's not nearly as large as the one in Colorado. Nor as well known," Jim explained. "But it's pretty famous among the people who firmly believe that aliens have visited the Earth. And some believe they still do.

It's rumored that a spaceship crashed there in 1897," Jim continued. "And the small guy flying it died in the crash and was buried in the local cemetery."

"That's pretty interesting," she said thoughtfully. "And what do you two gentlemen think about it? Since both of you have spent probably thousands of hours in the skies, have either of you seen one of these UFOs?"

"I can speak for both of us on that," Gene volunteered. "The answer is no. We haven't. But there are a lot of things neither of us has seen. And as my friend Jim is fond of saying, 'I've been to three county fairs, two goat ropings, and a midget mud wrestling contest, and I've never seen one.'"

As the twins looked at Jim, wondering why he would say something like that, he jumped in to say, "That's a little out of context. I usually say that when I'm looking at something so strange that it challenges the imagination."

"Now, what would challenge your imagination?" Marie asked, smiling. "I thought all of your world travels to exotic places would have prepared you for just about anything."

"Okay, I'll give you a quick example," Jim told her as he looked around. "A couple of months back, I had a trip to New York. We landed at LaGuardia airport.

It was my leg to fly back to DFW, so while the Captain did the walk-around the airplane, I went up to the terminal area to get the paperwork for the trip," he continued. "While I was there, I noticed five very beautiful ladies dressed in evening gowns.

At first glance, I didn't notice anything strange, other than anyone wearing an evening gown on a flight was definitely new to me," Jim said, trying not to laugh. "Then, on about the third time I looked at them, I noticed their hands. And their Adam's apples."

"Let me guess," Seppa jumped in saying. "Drag queens."

"Correct," Jim said, nodding. "And I'll admit, I'd never seen men look so good as women. Hell, I hadn't seen many women that looked that good."

"So, did you tell your Captain when you got back to the airplane?" Marie asked.

"Nope," Jim answered, smiling. "However, since it was my leg, I was supposed to stand in the cockpit door and greet the passengers as they got on.

"So, I just told the Captain that I had seen some of the most beautiful women in the world dressed like they were attending a black-tie event at the White House," Jim said, barely containing a laugh. "I suggested that he stand in the door and greet them as they got on."

"Did he?" Julie asked.

"Of course," Jim answered. "And as he stood there anticipating their entry, I damn near peed my pants, trying not to laugh out loud.

"Anyway, when they got close to the entry onto the plane, his face lit up, and the biggest smile you've ever seen appeared on his face," Jim said, laughing. "Then, as they slowly got closer to the plane, he realized what they were."

"What did he say then?" Julie asked, grinning.

"He calmly stepped into the cockpit, took his seat, turned to me, and said, *Lashley, you're the biggest asshole I've ever had the displeasure to meet.*"

"What happened after that? Did you get into any trouble?" Seppa asked, laughing.

"No," Jim answered. "A couple of minutes later, he turned to me smiling and said, *I'll get you back for that, you know.*"

"Did he?" Marie asked.

"No, and I haven't flown with him since then," Jim told them. "I was taken off the next trip, which was the last one of the month, for some training thing. He probably was, too.

But I do keep an eye out for him," he finished as Aurora smiled as she shook her head and left.

Chapter Thirty-Five

Moments later, Aurora returned, wheeling in a small cart with their lobster scampi and several side dishes, saying, "Anthony says he hopes you'll enjoy the meal, and he'll try to join you for an after-dinner drink."

Conversation then lagged as everyone enjoyed their meals. As the plates began emptying, Anthony finally came in smiling and said, "Well, it looks as if the scampi was, as Jim says, just fine!"

Jim shook his head, smiling, and declared, "Anthony, I'm going to change my *just fine* to *mighty fine*."

Anthony looked at Gene quizzically and asked, "Is that truly much of an improvement?"

"Definitely," Gene answered, wiping his lips with a napkin. "Probably one of the highest praises I've ever heard Jim give … on anything."

"Then, with your permission, I'll pull up a chair and join you in a small drink as soon as Aurora brings it in," Anthony said, sliding a chair from a nearby table between the twins.

He had barely sat down when she came through the connecting doorway with a silver tray bearing seven tulip-shaped cognac glasses and a bottle of Courvoisier L'essence Cognac.

"Ah, my lovely Aurora," Anthony said as she sat the tray in front of him. "Your timing is immaculate. Please get a chair and join us."

Jim rose from his chair and said, "Please, Ma'am, take my seat. I'll get another."

"Such a gentleman," she cooed as Jim held the chair for her. "Pay attention, Tony, you could learn some manners."

Jim pulled a chair over and sat to the right of Marie as Anthony poured the glasses one-third full. As he passed them, he said, "It's such a pleasure to have my beautiful family and good friends together."

As the last glass arrived at Aurora's place, he continued raising his glass, "To family. To friends. To the good life. Carpe Diem!"

As everyone looked at each other and raised their glasses, repeating "Carpe Diem," Marie leaned over and whispered, "Carpe Diem," as they tapped their glasses.

"So, Gene, what do you have on your agenda for the next few days?" Anthony asked, setting his glass down.

"I've got to go back to Virginia in the morning," Gene answered. "The company is having some issues with one of our contracts down in Mexico, and I'm hoping that I can resolve it without having to go down there myself."

"What about you, Jim?" Anthony asked, turning to look at him. "Are you going back into the *Friendly Skies*?"

"Not for a few more days, sir," Jim answered. "Mostly, I'll hang around the house and do a few chores."

"Then you'll have time to come back and join us again," Anthony said. "As you heard Aurora say, *I should learn some manners*. So, consider yourself obligated."

"Oh, Nonno," Julie said, laughing, "I'm pretty sure Jim nor anyone else has enough time to change you."

"And we wouldn't want for you to change anyway," Seppa chimed in.

"The young, what do they know?" Aurora said, smiling at Anthony. "But I guess I'm so used to his boorish behavior I'd be lost without him."

"Now you see why I love this lady," Anthony said, reaching for the half-empty bottle. "So, I think maybe I'll have just a wee bit more and toast my lovely wife before I head back to the kitchen. Anyone else?"

"Not I," Gene said, shaking his head. "I still have plenty and have to drive Jim home and then over to Dallas to my hotel."

"I will!" both girls shouted in unison, raising their glasses.

"No, you won't!" Marie said, shaking her head. "I told you, one glass of wine. And maybe a small glass of Cognac. You finish your drinks and then help Mom clear the table."

"Sorry, girls," Anthony told them. "I sometimes get carried away since I get to see you so seldom. Next time, leave your mother at home, and we'll do whatever we wish."

"You see the conspiracies I have to deal with?" Marie said, smiling and looking at Jim. "Impossible!"

"I should be so lucky," Gene said, setting his empty glass down. "I remember all the times when I got to hang out with my grandfather and all my cousins. Now, I've got some very, very, good friends … like Jim here. But there's nothing like family."

"I am blessed," Anthony said with a nod. "Now, I hope you'll include my family in your list of good friends."

"That's a certainty," Gene said with a glance at Jim. "Now, if you'll accept my deepest thanks and appreciation for an excellent meal, I have to leave. But I'm looking forward to my next visit."

As everyone rose, Gene walked around to shake Anthony's hand and say goodbye to the twins. Finally thanking Marie for the invitation, he raised Aurora's hand and gave it a light kiss, saying, "Good night, everyone."

"I'll walk Jim out," Marie said as Jim shook Anthony's hand. "Girls, get to work."

Chapter Thirty-Six

Jim had barely taken a sip of his first cup of coffee the next morning when the doorbell rang. Getting out of his recliner, he headed to the door, wondering who would be coming by this early in the morning.

Opening the door to see Gene, he asked, "Couldn't sleep? Get the time zones screwed up?"

"None of the above," Gene said, stepping into the house. "But I figured you'd be up and that you'd want to hear a little news."

"Coffee while you give me the news?" Jim asked, heading for the kitchen.

"Sure," Gene said, following him.

"Is this more oyster information or Jack Robertson?" Jim asked, pouring a cup.

"Oyster," Gene answered, taking the cup from Jim. "Let's sit at the table so I can spread out some papers."

"Have a seat," Jim replied, sitting down at the end of the table.

Gene stood beside Jim and started laying out organizational charts and family connections, saying, "Here are those who we believe are the main players in the distribution of fentanyl through the Oyster Company.

Starting at the source in Mexico, you'll see Ruben Guzman Zambada, known as 'El Disenos, which means The Machete," Gene told him, pointing to the name at the top of the chart. "He's the man who controls the operation. From bringing the fentanyl in from China to deciding how much goes where he runs the organization with mostly members of his extended family.

His sister, Juanita, is married to Jesus Martinez," Gene continued, following the chart with his finger. "Jesus's sister Margarita is married to Ricardo Guzman.

Another of Guzman's sisters, Maria, is Jason's wife," Gene said as he straightened up and sipped his coffee. "Another sister, Rosa, is married to Michael Gilliad, who's more or less the end of the management line.

We've looked into the people who are in the various companies Gilliad controls, and they are usually some distant cousins or married to another member of the Zambada line," Gene finished, finally taking a seat at the table.

As Jim finished following the chart, shaking his head, he asked, "What's the connection with Maria's Fortune? I can't believe this El Disenos would allow an outsider to control such a vital link in the chain. And the same for whoever's bringing it to him from Mexico?"

"Brothers to Ruben," Gene answered. "As far as the company can tell, that's their only connection, driving the boats."

"What's Black Water's plan?" Jim asked, getting up to bring the coffee pot to the table.

"They've assigned the Mexico operation, and the international water operation, basically Maria's Fortune, to Dark Water," Gene told him as Jim refilled his cup.

"Our current plan is to destroy both Maria's Fortune and the Mexico boat the next time they meet at sea," Gene finished.

"Does El Disenos have other avenues of distribution if we disrupt this one?" Jim mused as he sat down.

"Definitely," Gene said, nodding. "He still has several different routes across the Mexico/US border from Texas to California.

We don't have the manpower to tackle all those avenues," Gene admitted. "We'll just pass our information to the Customs and Border Patrol people."

"So, we're going to handle from Jason and or Maria down through Gilliad," Jim ventured. "Is that as deep as we'll go?"

"Yes," Gene answered. "We'll provide the DEA with the information and coordinate with them as far as timing on our operations."

"Do we have any proof that the Oyster Company is in the fentanyl distribution?" Jim asked, sitting back and looking at Gene. "I can't imagine the company ordering hits on so many people without absolute proof."

"That's been taken care of," Gene told him. "I'll explain that later. It was pretty ingenious."

"If we have the proof, what's my role going to be in this?" Jim asked, taking his empty cup to the sink.

"Maria, Jason, and Gilliad," Gene informed him. "Since they are all in Galveston, the company is leaving them to you."

"How much time do I have before we move?" Jim asked as he thought about being assigned to kill his first woman.

"Approximately three weeks," Gene answered. "I'm waiting for our operatives in Mexico to get their plan ready for my approval, and then we'll marry that with our plan for the domestic operations."

"What about the people running the bottom of the distribution chain?" Jim asked.

"Since most of them are spread across the entire country, I'm working with an agent at each of their locations," Gene answered. "I'll coordinate your plans with theirs to make sure the timing is synchronized.

Now, since I've made your day with this simple task, how about if I take you to breakfast and discuss Jack Robertson?" Gene asked, taking his coffee cup to the sink.

Chapter Thirty-Seven

"Which way?" Gene asked as they pulled away from Jim's house.

"Head north on Belt Line," Jim told him. "Then make a right on the frontage road when you come to Highway 80."

"Where are we heading?" Gene asked as he took the quickest route to Belt Line.

"Denny's," Jim answered with a slight smile.

"What do you find so special about Denny's?" Gene asked as he turned north on Belt Line Road.

"Well, this one is always open, always clean restrooms, and I like their menu," Jim answered. "And their prices are reasonable.

Yes, I could get a good chicken fried steak and eggs from a lot of places," Jim continued. "And maybe pay twice as much. But you know what? The next day, after your third cup of coffee, that seven-dollar breakfast from Denny's looks exactly like the fourteen-dollar breakfast from some other place."

"You should have been a poet," Gene said as they saw Highway 80 just ahead. "Such a way with words."

After being seated and placing their orders, Gene asked, "Now, are you ready to discuss Jack Roberston?" "Later," Jim said, shaking his head. "First, I want to hear about this *ingenious* distribution method of fentanyl."

"Okay," Gene said as he looked around the restaurant. "Remember those shells that were placed on the conveyor belt so carefully?"

"Yes," Jim answered. "I think they looked like they were heading toward the unused section of the building that Jason said was used for overflow if necessary."

"That's correct," Gene agreed, nodding. "Well, we picked up some very interesting conversations from monitoring Jason's phone.

It seems that after hours, a special team of four men, all distant family members, comes in and cleans those shells," Gene continued. "Needless to say, that piqued our interest. So, we began monitoring their phones.

Pretty soon, we learned that those shells were scrapped, steam cleaned with a very high-pressure system, rinsed with a chlorine solution, and stored in a locked area within that room," Gene said as the waiter arrived with their meals.

"Maybe very strange, but I don't see the connection yet," Jim said, shaking Tabasco generously on the gravy covering his chicken fried steak.

"Just be patient," Gene told him as he broke the yokes of his eggs. "When Maria's Fortune comes in, these same four guys with ten others come to work the oysters they brought in.

The ten workers do pretty much as any oyster operation in the area where we watched the people working while we were there," he continued. "But the four family members work in the rear area with the shells that have been cleaned the week before."

"Are the shells involved in the distribution?" Jim asked, trying to envision the operation.

"Yes," Gene said, smiling. "As a matter of fact, they are the key to the distribution. When the oysters are unloaded at the Oyster Company, there are several sacks full of special *'oysters.'*

These sacks, which weigh about fifty pounds each to simulate the other sacks of real oysters, are delivered to the rear area," Gene explained.

"There are empty shells glued to the inside of the sack to make it appear to be a sack of oysters, but within the sack are bags of fentanyl pills," Gene said, sitting back to give Jim time to see where this was going.

"So, these four guys working in the back are opening the special sacks, taking out the fentanyl, and putting it in the shells from before?" Jim asked incredulously.

"Exactly," Gene said, nodding. "The bags of fentanyl contain individual packets weighing about two ounces. They then put these packets in each oyster shell, glue it shut, and put all of them into sacks that will weigh about fifty pounds each.

Then they will be shipped out to the companies Michael Gilliland runs," Gene explained.

"Just how much are we talking about?" Jim asked, shaking his head in amazement.

"Here's the math," Gene answered. "Twenty-eight grams in an ounce, 448 grams in a pound at two hundred dollars a gram is about ninety thousand dollars a pound.

That makes almost nine million dollars for a hundred pounds or four and one half million for each fifty-pound sack," he explained. "If they send one sack to each of the twelve companies under Gilliad, that's almost fifty-six million dollars.

Now imagine how much that is if they send out a shipment every week," Gene said, looking at Jim do the mental math.

"You're talking about almost three billion dollars a year," Jim finally said, sitting back.

"Maybe a little less," Gene told him. "But it's definitely more than the salary of the average oysterman."

"How do they determine the *special* oyster sacks from the others?" Jim asked as he returned to eating his breakfast.

"There's a special red string in the thread that sews up the bottom of the sack," Gene answered, putting another squirt of ketchup on his hash browns. "All of the sacks have a metal seal with a tag showing their destination. The seal will let the company know if any sack has been opened."

"So now we know how they operate," Jim said, dipping a piece of toast into the gravy. "What do we do with the information?"

Chapter Thirty-Eight

Just as they were leaving Denny's, Gene's phone rang. Answering it as they got to the Suburban, he simply told the caller thanks and hung up.

"Well, it's started," he said as they got in the car. "That was Black Water letting me know that Maria's Fortune just pulled out of port early this morning and is headed to sea."

"Are they sure she's meeting the Mexico boat?" Jim asked as they pulled out of the parking lot.

"Absolutely," Gene assured him. "Our source in Mexico verified that boat left within thirty minutes of Maria's Fortune departing."

"So, what's going to happen?" Jim asked as they headed south on Belt Line.

"There's going to be an accident at sea," Gene replied, smiling. "There will be simultaneous explosions when the two boats get within ten feet of each other.

Charges were placed in the engine compartments of both boats, and they are rigged to blow when the phones connected to them are called," Gene continued. "Our satellite will let us know when they meet, and a call will be placed from Quantico to both phones."

"How long until they meet?" Jim asked as they drove south on Belt Line.

"Probably two days," Gene answered.

"Just a side note, in case you didn't know," Gene said as they arrived at Jim's house. "Every satellite we've sent up over the last few years has eyes. From communication satellites to those used for GPS, we're watching.

Additionally, they're maneuverable within an ever-increasing range," he finished shutting off the engine. "That expands our ability to monitor every person we choose to watch."

"So, what does that do to my timeline regarding Jason and the other two?" Jim asked, leading the way into the house.

"Probably less than a week now," Gene told him as they took seats in the living room.

"All this does is put pressure on El Desinos," Gene explained. "He'll lose fifty-six million dollars when those ships go down. And the distributors here in the States will be screaming about their part of the losses, not to mention the street dealers will start looking for other sources.

That alone will be a major hit to their business," Gene said. "Adding pressure to find replacement boats, as well as crews, could just cause mistakes that we and the government can use to our advantage."

"Glass of tea?" Jim asked, getting up.

"Coffee, if it's still warm," Gene said, following him into the kitchen.

"Microwave," Jim told him, pouring a cup. "The best invention since the handkerchief."

"You're comparing the microwave to a snot rag?" Gene asked, laughing.

"What did the man do before the handkerchief?" Jim asked, putting the coffee into the microwave and setting the time.

"Never mind," Gene told him, shaking his head. "Sometimes it's best to just let you ramble. But handkerchief?"

"Sometimes I guess I do," Jim agreed, handing the cup to Gene. "I don't always seem to have that little switch in my brain that disengages my mouth when it should."

Filling a tall glass with ice, Jim took a pitcher of tea from the refrigerator and poured it full, saying, "Since you've managed to destroy the next week's supply of fentanyl, do you have any plans for what we know is either headed to the streets or already there?"

"Unfortunately, if we disrupt that supply entirely, it will raise suspicions, and we might not be able to shut down the major players."

"How many people would die because of our inaction if we don't?" Jim asked as they returned to the living room.

"We're not sure," Gene answered somberly. "We don't have any accurate statistics, but it's estimated that there are about a thousand overdoses every year.

But it's climbing rapidly," he continued. "Over the last ten years, the CDC estimates an annual growth rate of over fifty percent using the known deaths and those suspected.

One of the problems is that the fentanyl is mixed with another drug, such as heroin, and that is listed as the reason for the overdose. Not the fentanyl," Gene finished.

"I guess it's the old adage, you've got to break a few eggs to make an omelet," Jim said, looking at Gene. "I guess I'd rather talk about that piece of shit Robertson's death than that of so many innocent people right now."

Chapter Thirty-Nine

"What are you thinking as far as how you want to proceed?" Gene asked as they returned to the kitchen for drink refills.

"I'd like to put a bullet in his face," Jim answered as he refilled his tea and heated another cup of coffee for Gene. "And I'd like for the last thing he sees is a full-blood Cherokee in a Dallas Police Officer uniform standing there smiling as I pull the trigger."

"I'm not sure we can arrange that," Gene commented as they returned to the living room. "Would a Comanche do as well?"

"It could be a member of the *Hacksaw Tribe,* as far as I'm concerned," Jim answered. "Or that infamous *Fucowee Tribe.*"

"I'll see what I can come up with," Gene told him, shaking his head. "Just don't hold your breath. You may be the closest thing to Cherokee we can get."

"I do want to use the same scenario we used when I shot the guy driving the car when Jennifer was killed," Jim told him. "Maybe we can't get the Indian, but at least he'll know why I'm shooting him. Especially when I tell him why I'm there."

"Okay, I'll start working on getting you the necessary items," Gene agreed. "We just had one of our agents join the Dallas Police Department, so that should help. Especially when it comes to the uniform and stuff."

"Why do we have people working within the police department?" Jim asked.

"We've always done so," Gene informed him. "Just as we have pilots, Flight Attendants, and even baggage handlers from the airlines. We also have people in the banking industry, financial institutions, and almost every walk of life.

Lots of them are just like you and more or less part-time," he continued. "Some are in those positions where we can get information that's unavailable to anyone outside of the corporation we're interested in. And as you know, most of our people will never fire a gun," he explained.

"But, like the dispatchers in your job, they're necessary to make the organization function. What we used to call 'shoe clerks' when we were in the Marines," he finished.

"How's getting personal habits info coming on Robertson?" Jim asked after thinking about the possibility of having a source within law enforcement.

"We've bugged his phone, his car, his house, and anyone he's contacted within the last week," Gene informed him. "The information we're getting is also providing us with a good look at the Aryan Nations groups he's been trying to join.

One thing we've learned is that the CIA has a plant within one of them," Gene continued. "That gives us a potential source if we need it. Maybe we can use him to set Mr. Robertson up."

"That would be a great help," Jim said, nodding. "Last time, we were just guessing when and where the guy was going and the route he would take.

This could narrow it down or even allow us to control every aspect of the meeting," he finished.

"Absolutely," Gene agreed. "That's going to be a big help since we're flying by the seat of our pants down in Galveston. If we could have absolute control up here, it would make it easier to make our plans for the Oyster Company."

"Okay, now that we have more or less come up with the framework for removing Robertson," Jim said. "How long do you think it will take El Disenos to get back in operation after his boats are sent to the bottom of the Gulf of Mexico?"

"Hell, he'll probably have a new boat to bring the fentanyl from Mexico that afternoon," Gene said, shaking his head. "And he's most likely got another brother or cousin that can drive it. It may take a day or two to acquire another oyster boat, but with his money, no more than a week."

"I guess the only thing that will slow him down is removing the Oyster Company and the distribution chain from there to the street," Jim said. "Even then, he has other avenues of getting his shit onto the streets."

"That's correct, except that his head is on the chopping block as well," Gene informed him. "Once we decide on the date, he will be the first to go. If we don't take him first, he'll rabbit, and we may not get another chance for some time."

"Even if you remove him, one of his family members that's familiar with the operation will step in and take over," Jim remarked. "If not one of them, some competitor."

"You're right," Gene agreed. "There's just too much money in the drug business for us to ever stop it. And I'm afraid this fentanyl issue will eclipse anything we've ever seen."

Chapter Forty

"Tell you what," Gene said after putting his coffee cup in the sink. "You call Marie, and I'll take you guys out to dinner tonight. Her choice of where we go.

I've got to go back to the hotel and do some work on a couple of loose ends, but I'll be back to pick you up by five o'clock," he finished. "Call me and let me know what she wants."

"Sure," Jim told him. "Her kids are down for a couple of days, and she doesn't get to see them often, so now she'll leave them home alone to have dinner with us? I don't think so."

"All she can do is say no," Gene offered.

"Nope, I don't want to put her on the spot," Jim replied. "I'll let you take me to dinner. Your choice of where we go."

"You're making a mistake," Gene said as Jim followed him down to the Suburban.

"I'll see you at five when you come to get me," Jim said as Gene got in the car.

"You can do better," Gene retorted as he started the car. "But you always were hard-headed. See you at five." Jim walked back into the house and began cleaning the kitchen before tackling the rest of the house. As he was trying to decide whether or not to start with his bedroom or the master bath, the phone rang.

"Hello," he answered, hoping it wasn't crew scheduling from American calling to offer him a trip.

"Jim, glad I caught you at home," Marie replied. "I have a favor to ask of you if you don't mind."

"Ask away," Jim told her. "I'm not an expert at favors, but I'm working on it."

"Now, this is rather short notice, but the girls are headed back to school tomorrow, and they wanted all of us to go to dinner tonight if that's all right with you," she told him.

"That sounds fine," Jim said, "but there's a slight problem."

"What's the problem?" Marie asked, wondering if she was pushing it too hard.

"I just promised Gene that I'd have dinner with him this evening," Jim answered.

"Well, ask him if he wants to join us," Marie argued. "That is if you want to have dinner with me, I mean us."

"I'll ask," Jim agreed, smiling. "But I can predict that his answer will be a resounding yes. I shouldn't say anything, but he offered to take us to dinner tonight before he went back to his hotel."

"And you told him no?" Marie asked.

"Yes, I did," Jim said. "Not because I didn't want to have dinner with you, but I figured that since the girls were going back to school tomorrow, you guys might want to spend the time together."

"Then I guess it's fortunate that the girls suggested we all go," Marie responded. "So, what time should we pick you up?"

"How about if we just meet you?" Jim suggested. "I'm not sure about Gene's schedule and whether or not he's flying back to Virginia tonight. Would that be okay?

"That works for me," Marie agreed. "Where would you like to go?"

"Why don't you let the girls pick it?" Jim suggested. "It was their idea, so it should be their decision."

"Good idea," Marie said. "But I'm guessing that they'll pick Bleachers Sports Grill. It's just off Arapaho Road, a little way past Jupiter heading east. It's been one of their favorites since they used to go there with their dad."

"That sounds fine with me," Jim replied. "What time?"

"How about six?" Marie suggested. "I think there's even a UNT football game on tonight if you're a fan."

"Not really," Jim told her. "But the girls would probably rather watch that instead of listening to us old folks talk. Gene and I will see you there at six."

Hanging up, he dialed Gene's number and, when he answered, said, "Well, I guess you'll get your wish for dinner."

"So, you came to your senses and called her," Gene said, smiling. "Good boy."

"Not so fast, Kemosabe," Jim told him. "She called me. Seems as if her girls wanted to go to dinner with us."

"Us? As in, you and I?" Gene joked.

"Sure, that's way up there on what college girls want to do on a Saturday night," Jim said. "Actually, they were referring to them with Marie and I."

"Then, by all means, go," Gene told him. "I'll just head back to Quantico a few hours earlier. The plane is at Love Field just waiting for me."

"No, you're invited too," Jim countered. "I told Marie that you and I had dinner plans, so she insisted that I bring you. You don't get off the hook that easy."

"Wouldn't have it any other way," Gene said, smiling. "What time?"

"Why don't you come by and get me around five as we planned," Jim suggested. "We can have a beer there before they arrive and discuss anything that you've learned since this morning."

"Sounds good," Gene agreed. "By the way, I guess you are aware that this is phase two of the '*Is this man good enough for our mother*' interview."

"I'll see you when you get here," Jim said shaking his head as he hung up.

Chapter Forty-One

After being seated at a table for six and ordering their beers, Gene said, "I'm sure you remember me saying that the CIA had a man in one of the Aryan Nations groups. Well, we've been given permission to use him."

"I meant to ask you at the time but forgot," Jim admitted. "But I thought there was only one Aryan Nation."

"You're mostly correct," Gene told him, nodding. "Maybe I should have said one of the white supremacist groups.

Here in Texas, there are mainly the Aryan Brotherhood of Texas and the Aryan Circle," Gene told him. "Two major Texas groups, the Aryan Society and the Aryan Brothers, merged to become The Aryan Brotherhood of Texas.

The Aryan Brotherhood of Texas then asked to form a chapter of the Aryan Nations in Texas but were denied," Gene explained. "Then the Aryan Circle came from other white supremacist gangs that were left out of the Aryan Brotherhood of Texas."

"Which group does our informant belong to?" Jim asked as the waitress brought their beers.

"The Aryan Circle," Gene said as he handed the waitress his credit card. "They're the smaller of the two, and it was easier for our guy's falsified prison record to pass scrutiny."

"What's our guy's name?" Jim asked, taking a sip of his beer.

"Let's just call him Bob for now," Gene answered. "If any hint of his real name or background ever leaked …"

"Understood," Jim said, nodding as he remembered what he had read about a guy who tried to join the Aryan Brotherhood of Texas. The guy was stabbed forty-two times for merely getting their tattoo when he wasn't a member. No telling what they'd do to an informant.

"Anyway, we've made initial contact, and Black Water did some modifications to his phone," Gene informed him. "I don't know much about that, but they can contact him without anyone who happens to get his phone knowing about it.

Something to do with the spelling of one of the names in his contact list," he said, shaking his head. "I've learned so much about how these damn cell phones can be manipulated … I'm not sure I even want one within fifty feet of me."

"I'm pretty sure that the program Bracer developed and installed on my phone is on all of ours," Jim commented. "But who's to say that some fat, pimple-faced, donut-eating computer nerd sitting in his mother's basement hasn't already cracked it."

"Cracked what?" came a voice behind Jim. "Pecans? Walnuts? Please don't say peanuts! Those are so hard to crack."

As Jim turned to see Marie standing behind him with the twins, he said, "You must be a Ninja. I certainly didn't hear you come up behind me."

Standing, he then said, "Ladies, please take a seat while my heart slows back to a normal beat."

Gene rose and bowed slightly, saying, "Once again, I have the pleasure of an evening with three of the loveliest ladies I've ever had the pleasure to meet."

"Always such a gentleman," Marie said as she took the seat to Jim's left. "Is that something you two learned in the Marines?"

"Oh yes," Jim answered as the twins took seats on either side of Gene. "We're known as 'The Few, The Proud, The Gentlemanly.' Haven't you heard that on the recruiting commercials?"

"Hey, that's better than that one that says, 'Aim High,'" Julie commented. "What does that mean? Shoot over their heads? Just shoot the tall ones?"

"What about being all you can be?" Seppa asked. "What if all you can be isn't very much? Let's say you're an anorexic midget with an IQ of twenty-seven. Is that all they want? I think all of the military needs to hire a good image consultant."

"What would you suggest for the Marines?" Gene asked her, smiling as he signaled for their waitress.

"How about 'We Mean, We Green, We be Marine,'" Julie answered as they laughed.

"How about 'Blue Sky, We Fly, They Die' for the Air Force," Seppa added, laughing with them. "I'm pretty sure those are better than what they've got."

"I hope you two aren't wasting my money if that's what you've learned in three years of college," Marie said, shaking her head. "I didn't send you there to become smart alecks."

"College isn't all about what you learn from books," Gene said as the waitress came to their table. "Developing the ability to think for yourself is more important, even if it's humorous jabs at our recruiting ads. That is *if* you pass the final exams on everything else.

Please put anything this table orders on my tab," he told her. "And my friend and I would also like another beer."

Chapter Forty-Two

A couple of hours later, after eating and discussing everything from the girls' after-college aspirations to Jim's experiences with American Airlines, Gene announced, "Well folks, again, I must thank you for letting me join you. It's been such a pleasure, but I must get back to Love Field.

"I have a meeting tomorrow morning, and I need to get up early and review a few things to ensure I don't make a fool of myself in front of my boss," he said as he signaled for the check.

"Please, let me have the check," Marie objected. "After all, I invited you."

"But I invited you before you invited Jim," Gene argued, smiling as he signed the check, adding a generous tip. "Even if you weren't aware, I was the first inviter."

"Then, at least let me leave the tip," Marie countered. "I mean, you didn't invite my girls, so …"

"Nope, it's all been taken care of," Gene replied, sliding his chair back. "And those two young ladies remind me of what it's like to see the world through the windshield instead of seeing most of it in the rearview mirror.

Now, I look forward to seeing all of you again, but I must really get going," he told them, looking at Jim.

"I'm afraid I've got to go with Gene," Jim said, sliding his chair back and standing. "As he said, this has been a most enjoyable evening."

"Well, if you both must go," Marie said, getting up, "at least let me walk you to your car."

"Now there's a chivalrous lady," Gene said as he stood telling the twins goodbye. "Next thing you know, you'll be teaching the girls how to curtsy."

"There's a relic from the past," Jim said, joining Gene in saying goodbye to the girls. "I thought that went out with wind-up watches and clocks."

"What's a curtsy?" Julie asked, giving Jim and Gene a hug.

"It's the reciprocal of a man bowing to a lady," Seppa answered as she gave Jim a hug. "I think I saw something like that in an old English movie with Earls and Ladies in Waiting, whatever that is."

"Ladies in waiting? Waiting for what?" Julie asked as Marie came around the table and took Jim's arm.

"I don't know," Seppa told her. "Maybe I'm a lady in waiting since I'm waiting for Mom to buy me a new car."

"And *in waiting,* you'll remain," Marie said as Jim led them toward the door. "Waiting until you graduate and get a job."

"I'll meet you at the car," Gene told Jim and Marie as they left the restaurant. "Good night, everybody. I hope we can do this again soon."

"I think I forgot my purse," Julie said, looking from Seppa to Marie. "I better go back in and see."

Seppa looked at Marie, smiling, and said, "I'll come with you. I'm pretty sure I left something inside, too."

As the girls went back in, Marie smiled at Jim and said, "I'm pretty sure they didn't leave anything inside."

"Probably not," Jim said as Marie put her arms around his neck. "Those two are about as subtle as a brick."

"But I'm glad they did," Marie said, standing on her toes kissing Jim. "Very glad."

Jim put his arms around her waist and pulled her close, returning her kiss. As he pulled back, he said, "Now that's about as good of an end to the evening as I've ever had."

"Guess I'll have to raise the bar next time," Marie said, looking deeply into his eyes. "When do you think the next time will be?"

"Soon. Very soon," Jim said, brushing a loose strand of hair from Marie's face. "Maybe next time without the crowd."

"I'll make sure of it," Marie replied. "At least I can make sure the girls are back in school."

"Those two are really something," Jim told her as he took her hand. "They're fun. But …"

"I think they're standing behind the door waiting," Marie said after taking a glance behind her. "Let's head for your car and see if they come back out."

"If they do, we'll go to where you parked," Jim suggested as the door to the restaurant opened. "I'm still not used to chivalrous ladies."

"Did you find your purse?" Marie asked as the girls came out and joined them.

"I just remembered that I left it back at Nonno's house," Julie answered, smiling at Seppa.

"In that case, I'll walk you ladies to your car," Jim said as Marie led the way. "I guess I'm not modern enough to let a lady walk me to my car. My Mother would be shaking her head at me if I were so rude. And Dad would slap me behind the head.”

“When will we get a chance to see you again?” Julie asked as they got to Marie’s car.

“You’re getting way too personal, young lady,” Marie said, lightly slapping her arm. “That’s none of your business.”

“I hope soon,” Jim said, laughing. “But it’s up to your mother. Regardless, I’ve enjoyed this evening with you and look forward to the next time.”

“Us, too,” Seppa said. “It’s about time for Mother to get out and have some fun.”

“Say goodnight, girls,” Marie said, turning to Jim. “You and Gene drive carefully. And tell him again thanks for the evening.”

Chapter Forty-Three

The following evening, as Jim was preparing dinner, the phone rang. Wiping his hands on the towel he had over his shoulder, he answered, "Hello."

"Got a couple of minutes?" Gene asked.

"Sure," Jim answered, turning off the burner beneath the simmering mixed vegetables he was heating. "What's up?"

"There's been an explosion at sea," Gene told him.

"Such a tragedy," Jim replied, smiling. "I hope there were plenty of life rafts in accordance with current seafaring regulations."

"Probably," Gene said. "But it appears that those life rafts and all hands went down with the ships."

"Well, I guess now we wait," Jim said, walking to the refrigerator and pulling out a Ziegen Bock.

"Yes, but probably not too long," Gene agreed. "They had a pretty regimented reporting system. If either boat didn't report in within a narrow time frame, word was sent to El Disenos."

"Do you think he knows he's lost his shipment by now?" Jim asked, walking outside.

"Probably not, but I'd bet by sunrise he's sent someone out to look for them," Gene answered. "And I'm sure he'll be calling either Maria or Jason to see if they know anything."

"Since we're monitoring his calls," Jim said knowingly, "we'll know within minutes of him knowing."

"Most assuredly," Gene agreed. "Now, have you been thinking about how you're going to handle the three targets?"

"As a matter of fact, I have," Jim answered, sitting down by the wrought iron table on his back porch. "And I think this little 'accident' will fit into my plans rather nicely."

"How do you plan on using it?" Gene asked.

"First, I have a couple of questions," Jim replied. "Earlier, I asked about using fentanyl on Jack. Then decided to just shoot him.

But, staying with the Old Testament theme, I've been thinking about using fentanyl to eliminate my targets," Jim continued. "First, can Black Water get me an aerosol that would deliver about five milligrams in a single shot?"

"Probably," Gene answered. "How do you plan on administering it?"

"Obviously, I have to be within an arm's length," Jim answered. "So, I'll need a couple of assistants to make sure I can handle the spray without hurting either myself or them."

"That's certainly doable," Gene said. "Now, how do you plan on getting the three of them together? Or do you plan on separate operations?"

"One operation," Jim answered. "If I can get the assistants I need, and if Black Water can do a little subterfuge, I think I can be in and out within an hour."

"What do you need us to do?" Gene asked, wondering what sort of operation Jim was planning.

"Since El Disenos will most certainly be looking for new boats and crews, I propose we insert another *family member* into the equation," Jim told him.

"Once El Disenos notifies Maria or Jason that he's arranged for new equipment and men, I want you to place another call," Jim explained.

"If Black Water can duplicate El Diseno's voice and make it appear that the call is coming from his phone, we can set up a meeting between them and the new member of the organization," Jim finished.

"What will El Disenos tell them?" Gene asked, thinking about the technology the company had recently developed.

"He'll tell them that the new guy will come down to make sure the new boat Captain doesn't have any problems with his end of the operation," Jim answered.

"And he'll tell them that for the next couple of weeks, the output must be doubled to make up for the losses they suffered when the boats went down," Jim continued.

"And you'll take care of the three of them during this meeting," Gene replied, nodding.

"Yes," Jim said. "If Black Water can supply the fentanyl and can give me the two men I need. But none of this will work unless you can convince the three people that it's on the order of El Disenos. I see that as the key."

"I'll get with the company and see what we can come up with," Gene told him. "And I guess it would help if the two assistants were of Hispanic origin."

"Most definitely," Jim agreed. "Spanish speakers would go a long way toward making this believable."

"I'll get to work on my end," Gene finally said. "Can you think of anything else you might need?"

"Not at the moment," Jim answered. "But if you folks there at Quantico have any suggestions, I'll welcome them."

"I'll get back to you in the morning," Gene said. "Timing on the phone call is going to be critical. We need to give El Disenos time to get his new boats and crews. But we can't wait too long after he talks to the Oyster Company before we call to inform them of the new member of the organization."

"I agree," Jim told him. "How much time do you think we have to implement this?"

"I don't think it will take more than two days for El Disenos to have the new boats and crew," Gene answered. "Then another couple of days to set everything in motion to get the next supply of fentanyl to the Oyster Company.

I'd plan on setting the meeting for four or five days from now," he continued. "But we'll know better once he learns of the unfortunate accident at sea.

And we can slide the meeting as we monitor their phones," Gene finished. "Flexibility is the key to success."

"I know the saying. And indecision is the key to flexibility," Jim told him. "The company took my first trip, but my flexibility ends in about six days when I have to go back to work."

"Let's not worry about that for now," Gene said. "I might be able to provide a little additional flexibility on that issue if it comes down to it."

"I know you can," Jim told him, thinking that the sudden change to his flying schedule was due to Dark Water's involvement. "I'll be waiting for an update when you learn what El Jefe is doing. Have a good evening, General."

"You, too," Gene said, smiling as he was hanging up. "And tell Marie the same when you talk to her later this evening."

Chapter Forty-Four

"What are your plans for the day?" Gene asked as Jim answered the phone the next morning.

"Wash the car, mow the yard, fall in love, get married, have kids, win the lottery, divorce the wife, give up half of my money, and move into a single wide in the trailer park by the railroad tracks," Jim answered walking back into the kitchen for more coffee. "How about you?"

"I'm on my way from Chicago," Gene told him. "I've got the two men we've assigned to help you with your problem. We'll be landing at Love Field in a little over an hour and be at your house shortly after that."

"Okay," Jim replied. "Why are you bringing them here?"

"I thought it would help if you three got together and worked out how you would handle the situation before you get to Galveston," Gene answered. "Just a little run-through of how you plan to use them, maybe get a little feedback from them if they see any flaws. And just a chance to meet the men you're working with."

"Sounds good," Jim replied. "Have you guys had breakfast?"

"No, but please don't tell me you want to go to Denny's again," Gene said, shaking his head.

"Do you know of any better place?" Jim asked, smiling. "If so, we'll go there. But you're buying if we do."

"It seems like I'm buying no matter where we go," Gene countered. "Would it be asking too much if you had a pot of coffee when we get to your house?"

"I'll have a fresh pot just for you," Jim told him. "And that snide remark about buying? You aren't buying; the company is. Don't think I haven't seen the credit card you always use."

"Benefits of the position," Gene replied, laughing. "We'll see you in about an hour and a half."

Jim was still washing the 'Vette when Gene pulled up in his typical black Suburban.

Watching everyone get out of the car, he turned off the hose and wiped his hands before walking down the driveway to greet them.

"General, good to see you again," Jim said, shaking his hand. "How long has it been, forty, maybe forty-eight, hours?"

"Guys, here's the pain in the ass you'll be working with," Gene said, turning to the two men with him.

"Jim, meet Javier Guzman and Rob Sproc," Gene said, introducing them.

Shaking each of their hands, Jim asked, "Rob Sproc? I've heard that name before, and you don't look Hispanic."

"My real name is Roberto," Rob told him. "My mom is from Guatemala, and my dad is gringo like you."

"Javier, are you any kin to Ruben Guzman Zambada, El Disenos?" Jim asked, shaking his hand.

"Not that I know of," he answered. "But I do know we have extended family down around Puerto Vallarta. And Guzman is a rather common name. As is Zambada."

"What has Gene told you so far?" Jim asked, leading them to the house.

"Only that we'll be helping you with three individuals involved with the fentanyl trade down in Galveston," Javier answered.

"That's the basics of the plan," Jim said as they followed him into the kitchen. "Let me get you guys some coffee, and we'll go out on the porch and work on some details.

Basically, I'm going to be administering five milligrams of fentanyl to each of the three," Jim told them as they sat around the table. "I'll need you to get there ahead of me and convince them that you're there to oversee the new boat Captain and see how they plan on increasing production due to the recent loss.

Once you get them into the conference room, I think having them on one side of the table and you on the other would be best," Jim continued.

"Tell them something about waiting for the new Captain to get there before getting into any details," Jim added. "Just try to put them at ease."

"No problem. We can handle that," Javier said, nodding and looking at Rob. "Rob's got an issue with fentanyl anyway since he had a member of his family overdose last year. That's why he jumped at the chance for this mission."

"Sorry to hear that," Jim told him. "I wish I could let you take care of these people yourself, but I don't want to risk anyone else handling the shit I'm going to shove up their noses."

"I'll be satisfied to just sit and watch them die," Rob said, nodding. "Besides, it's more appropriate to watch them suffer for the five or so minutes it takes for them to die than a quick bullet through the brain."

"That's part of why I've planned it this way," Jim told him. "Let them see what their crap is doing to everyone that uses it."

Chapter Forty-Five

After going over more details and trying to cover all of the 'what ifs' while having breakfast, they returned to Jim's house to finalize their plans as best they could.

"Any more questions?" Jim asked as they returned to the porch. "Suggestions?"

"Not that I can think of," Javier answered looking from Rob back to Jim.

"Me neither," Rob said. "But things always have a tendency to go off the rails at the most inopportune time."

"That they do," Jim said as Gene walked away, answering his phone. "But as long as you can keep them in their chairs until I walk in, we can handle anything that comes up."

"I forgot to ask," Javier said suddenly. "Do you think any of them will be armed?"

"Probably not," Jim answered. "But, as Rob said, things sometimes go off the rails."

"Do you think we should search them?" Rob asked.

"No, that would seem extremely out of place given the circumstances," Jim said, shaking his head. "I want them completely unaware of any threat."

"Even if they are armed, I'm sure we can handle it," Javier said. "They'll be sitting down, and we'll have our weapons already out when you come in."

"I agree," Jim said as Gene came back to the table. "They'll be turning to see me as I come into the room, and you'll have a chance to bring your guns up while they're distracted."

"Well, gentlemen," Gene announced, taking his seat. "The word's out. Ruben just called Maria asking what the hell was going on."

"That's pretty much what we expected, isn't it?" Jim asked. "Two days?"

"Yes," Gene agreed. "Now all we have to do is wait for him to get the new boats."

"How's the company coming with *our call* from Ruben informing them about Javier coming down?" Jim asked.

"Damn near undetectable," Gene answered. "They put every phone call or other recording of his voice into their computer system and analyzed every word.

The guy who will make the call has years of experience mimicking other voices and has been practicing for the last couple of days," he continued.

"Additionally, there are always some background noises when Ruben calls," he explained. "We'll have those same noises when our call is made.

The folks at Quantico have made several practice runs, and any slight deflection in the voice is undetectable with the background noise," Gene finished. "When they played recordings of Ruben and our man to several people, nobody could tell the difference. Also, the spectrograph comparison would hold up in any court in the world. As I said, damn near undetectable."

"I think we're as ready as we'll ever be," Jim said, nodding. "That is if the nasal spray stuff is going to be ready."

"It's ready," Gene assured him. "They've basically taken a normal nasal inhaler and added a small flexible shield that will prevent any of the fentanyl from coming back out of their nose onto your hand as long as you insert it fully."

"One other thing," Jim said. "Are the guns Javier and Rob will be bringing clean? Just in case they have to use them."

"They'll match ones that were used in Chicago last year in a shootout between two drug dealers," Gene answered. "If they have to shoot, the bullets will be a perfect match. We'll preload the magazine and make sure there are no fingerprints on the actual projectile. As unlikely as it is that a fingerprint would survive the shot, we don't want to take the chance.

Now, if there aren't any more questions or potential problems we need to discuss, I have to get back to Quantico and, therefore, need to pass through Chicago to take these guys home," Gene announced, getting up.

"Thanks for coming down," Jim told Javier and Rob as they walked to Gene's Suburban. "Please don't hesitate to give me a call if you think of anything we need to take a second look at. Even if it's something as minor as the sitting arrangements when you take them into the conference room, let's talk about it before we get there."

"You'll have another opportunity to go over any final issues the night before," Gene informed them. "I've made reservations at the same hotel where we stayed, and we'll be coming by to pick you up at Love Field on our way down."

"When you say 'we,' is that the royal 'we,' or are you coming with us?" Jim asked as they got to the car.

"I'm coming with you," Gene answered, opening the car door. "I'll be on the line with Quantico monitoring Dark Water's operations as well as others across the country.

Someone has to be in a position to make instant decisions about each of the operations that are taking place simultaneously," Gene said, getting into the car. "And that someone is me."

"Couldn't you do that from your office in Virginia?" Jim asked as Javier and Rob got in the car.

"I could," Gene replied. "But your operation is sort of the linchpin to the timing. If Dark Water is on time with their operations in Mexico, we shouldn't have any problems with word leaking out here in the States.

So, I want to be able to see the exact minute things happen down in Galveston, and then I can make adjustments to the others if necessary," he said, starting the car. "Any objections?"

"Nope," Jim said, smiling. "I just thought you wanted to have a chance to hang out with me again."

Shaking his head, Gene gave Jim a final glance and drove away.

Chapter Forty-Six

Jim finished most of the chores he had assigned himself and decided that the remaining few could be put off until tomorrow.

Finally giving in to the desire to talk to Marie, he dialed her number, hoping she was at home and not at the restaurant. When she did answer, he was at a loss for words but finally managed to say, "Hey."

Marie waited a couple of seconds and repeated, "Hey."

After waiting another second or two, she asked, "Is that all you called to say?"

"No," Jim answered. "I guess I was sort of surprised when you answered the phone."

"Who did you think would answer it?" Marie asked.

"I mean, I didn't know if you were home or at the restaurant," Jim told her. "Maybe I should have thought about what I wanted to say before I called."

"Okay, have you figured it out yet?" Marie asked, enjoying Jim's obvious discomfort.

"Yea, um, are you doing anything this evening?" he finally asked.

"Not yet," Marie answered. "What do you have in mind?"

"I was thinking about cooking a couple of steaks," Jim suggested. "Then maybe go out to a movie."

"Okay, the steak part sounds fine. What did you have in mind for a movie?" she asked.

"I don't know," Jim admitted. "I haven't been to the movies in years and don't have a clue what's new or worth watching. How about you pick?"

"Do you have a VCR?" Marie asked.

"Yeah, I'm not sure it still works, but I've got one," Jim answered.

"Okay, here's my pick," Marie replied. "I'll stop by the movie store and get something. I'll surprise you."

"That sounds good to me," Jim said, relieved that he didn't have to make the decision. "How about six or six-thirty?"

"Six-thirty works for me," she told him. "Can I bring anything else?"

"Just a smile," Jim said, finally relaxing. "I think I have everything else."

"A microwave?" Marie asked. "Preferably clean?"

"Of course, how do you think I'm cooking the steaks?" Jim joked as he began to relax.

"I can almost believe that," Marie said, laughing. "I mean for the popcorn, dummy."

"I'm not sure if I have any," Jim told her. "I need to go get some things for dinner anyway. What kind do you like?"

"Things for dinner or popcorn?" Marie continued to joke.

"Popcorn," Jim answered, wondering why she was giving him such a hard time.

"I know that," Marie told him, laughing. "I'll bring the popcorn. Anything else?"

"No, that'll do it, I think," Jim answered. "I'll see you at six-thirty."

"Looking forward to it," Marie said, laughing before hanging up. "And I like my steak micro-waved to a delicious rubber-like consistency."

As the phone went dead, Jim decided to do another quick walk-through to make sure the house was reasonably clean. Especially the microwave.

After returning from the grocery store, Jim was rinsing the asparagus and potatoes when the phone rang. Hoping it wasn't Marie canceling, he answered apprehensively, "Hello?"

"Got an update for you," Gene said. "Ruben has his boats. We heard him finalizing a deal for one in Tampico, and Jason has located one in Port Arthur that's just come up for sale."

"How's he going to get that boat and have time to do any oyster harvesting before they run into more supply problems?" Jim asked.

"They're buying the oysters in Mexico and bringing them in the boat that brings the fentanyl," Gene answered. "That saves them about four days."

"What's the timeline now?" Jim asked, knowing that he'd probably be leaving tomorrow.

"We'll pick you up around noon tomorrow," Gene answered, confirming his suspicions. "I'll have the product and a weapon for you. Black Water is going to make *our* call to Jason around noon tomorrow also. The meeting will be scheduled for early the next morning."

"What would happen if the real El Disenos tries to call while we're talking to Jason? Or calls later?" Jim asked.

"We're controlling his phone," Gene told him. "We can shut it down anytime we need to. As far as he knows, he dials, but his calls never go anywhere. And he can't receive calls from anyone calling him.

Not to mention the fact that he'll be dead when you have your meeting, so you won't have to worry about him interrupting you," Gene added. "Now, if you have any more questions, please hold them until tomorrow. I've got a lot of work to get done, making sure everyone is ready to move when you walk into the conference room."

Chapter Forty-Seven

Hearing the doorbell ring, Jim glanced at the clock on the stove and headed for the front door.

"Marie, right on time," he said, opening the door.

"Always," she said, shifting the bag she was carrying to her left hand and hugging him with her right arm.

"My Dad drilled it into me when I was just a kid that it's better to be twenty minutes early than one minute late," she added, following Jim into the kitchen. "Where should I put this?"

"Just set it on the counter," Jim said as he looked around to see if there were any obvious areas he hadn't at least wiped down.

Setting the sack on the counter, Marie reached in, pulled out a bottle of Merlot, and sat it down.

Seeing her put the wine on the counter, Jim said, "I told you that you only need to bring a smile. You didn't have to bring wine."

"Papa was afraid you'd have some cheap-ass wine and wanted to give you this bottle," Marie said, taking the Pop Secret Butter Lovers popcorn out of the sack but leaving the movie inside. "And this wine runs north of ten dollars just about anywhere in the world where it's sold."

"Really? How far north?" Jim asked, picking up the bottle.

"Sometimes as much as two dollars," Marie answered with a smile. "And I'm guessing that two dollars is about all you ever spend on wine."

"I'll have you know that I've tasted some of the most famous five-dollar wines in the country," Jim replied, smiling. "But yet I never let anyone know that I am a world-renowned wine connoisseur sought by the most prestigious vineyards in Texas."

"Does Texas have any prestigious vineyards?" Marie asked, laughing.

"I'm not sure," Jim said taking a bottle of Jack Daniel's from the cabinet. "My secretary handles all the minor details and scheduling my appearances. Would you care for a pre-dinner beverage?"

"I could be persuaded to join you in one, perhaps Jack and Coke?" she answered.

"Ah, a lady after my own heart," Jim said, taking down two glasses.

Filling them with ice and setting them on the counter, he took a can of Coke from the refrigerator and asked, "Strong or candy ass?"

"Half and half, my good man," she answered, taking one of the glasses from the counter. "How about you?"

"I'm more of a fifty percent Coke, fifty percent Jack type of guy," he told her, smiling. "I've never liked that half-and-half stuff."

Pouring both glasses with Jack Daniel's and then adding Coke, she handed one to Jim and said, "To a wonderful evening with a handsome gentleman."

Tapping her glass, Jim said, "And a lovely lady.

I'll go get the mesquite started," Jim said after taking a sip and heading for the back door. "We'll have a few minutes before I put the steaks on so if you'll join me, we can enjoy the evening air from my veranda."

"Wow," Marie said, following Jim. "You must really be a world-renowned connoisseur to have your personal veranda. Connoisseur of what is yet to be determined, though."

"Hey, it sounded better than let's sit on the back porch until the grill's ready," Jim said, putting some lighter fluid on the split mesquite pieces already in the grill.

"What's the old saying about lipstick and a pig?" Marie said as she sat down, watching Jim.

"I have no idea," Jim said, taking the chair across the table from her. "My friends never discuss their dating habits. Ungentlemanly-like, you know."

"Not to change the subject, but is there anything I can do while you're cooking the steaks?" Marie asked.

"The potatoes are in the oven, the salads are in the refrigerator, so the only other thing is the asparagus," Jim answered. "I'll get the skillet for you if you'd like to take care of that."

"A waste of my culinary skills, but I'd be happy to," she said, taking one of Jim's hands. "I don't suppose you have any mushrooms to sauté, do you?"

Chapter Forty-Eight

After they had eaten, the table cleared, and they were enjoying a small glass of Quarante Tres on the porch. Jim finally asked, "What movie did you bring?"

"Still a surprise," Marie said as she sipped her liqueur. "You just have to wait and see when I start it."

"You know I could have looked in the bag while you weren't watching me," Jim told her, smiling.

"I knew you wouldn't do that," Marie told him. "Just like you'd never look in my purse if I left it on the counter. You're not like that."

"Then I guess I'll just have to wait," Jim gave in. "But if it's not good, I may never let you pick the movie again."

"So, you're planning on an *again*?" Marie asked, grinning.

"Depends on the movie," Jim said, laughing as he finished his drink. "Now, if you'd finish that last drop, I'll go start the popcorn while you put the movie in the VCR. Otherwise, I'll know what it is."

"Deal," Marie told him as she tilted her glass to get the few remaining drops. "Just don't let it burn. I hate burned popcorn."

"How about a Dr Pepper with your popcorn?" Jim asked, getting up.

"Sounds good," Marie answered, standing and handing Jim her glass. "I'll run to the lady's room while you start the popcorn."

Grabbing the bag from the counter as she headed from the kitchen, she said, "I'll meet you in the living room."

A few minutes later, when they were sitting on the couch facing the TV, Marie asked, "Ready?"

"Have been for hours," Jim answered. "The suspense is almost unbearable."

Pointing the remote at the VCR, Marie started the movie. As the black background with white writing scrolled down the screen and then the Lady Liberty figure holding a torch logo of Columbia Pictures appeared, Jim leaned slightly forward and then said, "I don't believe it. You got Dr Strangelove!"

"I guess that means you like my choice," Marie said, grinning as the opening scene of distant mountaintops above the deck of clouds appeared.

"One of my favorites," Jim exclaimed. "I haven't seen this in years."

"I almost got a vampire movie," Marie admitted. "But I wasn't sure if you liked scary movies."

"Love them," Jim told her as they watched the iconic scene of a B52 being refueled by a KC135 and the credits appeared.

"But this is great. I love Peter Sellers," he continued, turning slightly to look at her.

"You know he played three roles in this movie," Marie informed him.

"I know," Jim said, nodding. "The British exchange guy, the President, and Dr Strangelove."

"I really liked the Pink Panther movies, too," Marie added as the credits disappeared and the movie began.

"Me, too," Jim whispered, watching the scenes of B52's change to the interior of a building.

When the movie ended, Marie leaned over and kissed Jim on the cheek, saying, "You know I said I'd have to raise the bar next time we spent the evening together."

"I remember," Jim said as she leaned on his shoulder. "And you have. This has been a terrific evening. Great food. A most magnificent wine, thank your dad for that, and a classic movie."

"That's not what I'm referring to," Marie said, sitting up and facing him.

Jim watched as she took the bag that had held the popcorn, wine and movie. Reaching into the bag, Marie pulled out a very skimpy red nightie.

"Maybe this will give you a hint," she said, smiling, holding it up.

"I may be a little slow at times," Jim said, turning off the TV and VCR, "but I'm pretty sure that means you don't want to drive home tonight."

"It's not that I don't want to drive home tonight," she corrected him. "It's that I want to spend the night here … with you."

"No matter how you say it, I think that's the best idea you've had since you picked the movie," Jim said, standing and helping her up.

"Now I'm being compared to an old movie," Marie joked as Jim led her down the hall to his bedroom.

Chapter Forty-Nine

The next morning, Jim woke early and quietly slipped out of the bed. Padding his bare feet to the kitchen, he had barely started the coffee when Marie came up behind him and wrapped her arms around his waist.

"Trying to slip out on me?" she asked teasingly.

"How do I slip out of my house?" Jim answered, turning in her arms. "I'd have nowhere to go."

"Then you must have been trying not to disturb me," she argued. "I'm trying to decide which I'd like better, you not disturbing me or cuddling. Tough choice."

"Ah, but you don't get coffee with cuddling," Jim reminded her.

"That does present a conundrum," Marie said, removing her arms. "But I believe the decision maker will be whether or not you have orange juice."

Jim walked to the refrigerator, took out a carton of orange juice, set it on the counter, and said, "Decision maker."

Getting two glasses and two cups from the cabinet above the countertop, he set them down and said, "Your decision … back to bed and cuddle or orange juice and coffee."

"The mood's broken," Marie said, pouring juice in both glasses. "Maybe next time."

"In that case, let's take the juice and coffee out on the porch," Jim said, filling both cups.

"What happened to the veranda?" Marie asked, taking a seat as they got outside.

"Oh, that was just to make a good impression," Jim answered, sitting across from her. "Now, it's just a porch."

"So that's the kind of man you are," Marie teased, taking a drink of her juice. "Promise a girl a veranda and then give her a porch."

"Well, in the dark, it could be mistaken for a veranda," Jim argued, smiling.

"You're a mess, Mr. Lashley," Marie said, taking one of his hands. "A real mess."

"And that's my best quality," Jim said, squeezing her hand. "I have other lesser qualities, but I'm pretty damn proud of being a mess. It's taken me years to attain my elevated level of messiness."

"You've done well, grasshopper," Marie said, laughing. "If there was a college degree in messiness, you'd have a Ph.D."

"I never got quite that far," Jim said, sitting back in his chair. "I barely got a two-year degree, and they had to use a few creative course adjustments even for that."

"I thought you had to have a degree to be a pilot in the Marines," she said. "Isn't that so?"

"Well, there was this special program during Vietnam when they were running out of pilots," Jim explained. "And my friend Gene, who was the General I met over there, is the reason I got to fly then and now for American Airlines."

"I never knew he was a General," Marie said. "I just thought you guys met over there and became friends."

"That's part of what happened," Jim told her. "But Gene's really the reason I've been given the chances I've had in life."

"It sounds like he's been a great friend," Marie said.

"More than just a friend," Jim said. "He's been behind most of my career. Both in the Marines and with American. Without his help, I'd probably be driving rock trucks for a living."

"Then I'll have to give him my special thanks next time I see the General," Marie said, getting up and coming around the table to sit in Jim's lap. "Because without him, you'd never have met me."

"First, please don't let him know you know he's a General," Jim said. "He's not the kind of guy who carries his rank after retirement.

And second, how do you know I wouldn't have met you anyway?" Jim said, brushing some hair from her face.

"Oh, I just don't think too many rock truck drivers would be coming into our restaurant," she answered, laying her head on his shoulder.

"Probably not," Jim agreed as Marie snuggled against him. "What do you have planned for the rest of the day?" "I'm going over to my house and see if I'm happy with everything they've finished on the remodeling," she answered, lifting her head. "What about you?"

"Gene's coming by to pick me up and go down to Galveston," he answered.

"What's happening down there?" Marie asked.

"His company is looking into a contract with an oyster company down there," Jim answered.

"Why does an oyster company need to contract security?" Marie asked, looking at Jim.

"Black Water also has a lot of expertise in computer security," Jim told her. "I've heard that's one of the fastest-growing areas in security these days."

"What do you know about computer security?" Marie asked. "I thought you were more of an advisor for stuff like guards or fences or something."

"You're correct," Jim said. "I'm more familiar with the physical security issues. And I'm dumb as a box of rocks when it comes to computer security. Or anything to do with a computer."

"Then why does Gene want you to come to Galveston?" Marie asked, frowning.

"I think it's just to make it look like we have a big team," Jim told her. "There are two more guys coming, and they may be the real computer people.

Or, Gene may just want someone who isn't a computer geek to talk to the company with him," Jim added.

"When will you be back?" she asked, laying her head back on his shoulder.

"I'm hoping sometime tomorrow afternoon," Jim answered. "Maybe you can squeeze me in for a look at your house and what you've done remodeling it.

And, if it's not too late after that, we can go have dinner at your dad's restaurant, and I'll get a chance to say *hi* to him and your mother," Jim finished as he kissed the top of her head.

Chapter Fifty

After Marie left, Jim went into the bedroom and took out his suitcase to pack it for the trip to Galveston. The lingering scent of Marie's perfume gave him pause, and a slight smile formed as he put a couple of pairs of socks and underwear in the suitcase.

When he had finished making the bed, he carried his suitcase out to the living room and turned on the TV to catch the latest news while he waited for Gene to tell him when to be at Love Field.

Almost thirty minutes into the commentary about some issue regarding the condition of the roads in some of the poorest neighborhoods of Dallas, the phone rang.

Checking the time, he was expecting it to be Gene. "Good morning," he answered.

"I believe you've already had a good morning, haven't you?" Marie asked.

"I guess I was expecting this to be Gene telling me when to meet," Jim explained.

"That's why I'm calling," Marie replied. "I wanted to apologize for something I did this morning."

"What was that?" Jim asked.

"I sort of crossed the line getting to your personal business," she told him. "I shouldn't have questioned you about why you were going to Galveston with Gene. That was none of my business."

"That's all right," Jim replied. "How your remodeling is going is none of mine either. But I think taking an interest in someone's life is only normal if you're trying to build a relationship."

"That makes me feel better, but I don't want to be nosey," she told him. "Especially when it comes to your friends."

"I appreciate that," Jim told her. "But I hope my friends soon become your friends. You've already impressed Gene, so don't be surprised if he takes an interest in you and your family."

"Well, good," Marie said, breathing a sigh of relief. "Give me a call when you get back, and I may be able to give you a very special tour of my home."

"That sounds like something I'd like," Jim said, grinning. "I'll give you a call as soon as I get home and clean up."

"I'll be waiting," she said before hanging up.

Almost immediately, the phone rang again, and Jim answered, "Hello?"

"I tried calling you a few minutes ago," Gene scolded. "We're taxing out and should be there in a little less than four hours. Can you be ready to jump on board as soon as we refuel?"

"No problem," Jim answered. "I'll be there."

"Good. And I guess your evening went well since you had a morning after phone call," Gene told him, laughing before hanging up.

"Son of a bitch," Jim thought, looking at his phone. *"That does it. I'm getting another phone for my personal use and pulling the battery out of this one unless I'm talking to that meddling rascal."*

A couple of hours later, Jim tossed his suitcase in his pickup and headed for Love Field. After having a little time to think about his conversation with Gene, he decided that Gene hadn't been using the phone to spy on him. It was just his intuition that he had been on the phone with Marie.

And changing his phone number for American Airlines and his other friends would be a pain in the butt.

"I guess it comes down to trust," Jim thought as he pulled into the parking lot at Love Field. *"And if there's one person in the world that I'd trust with my life, it's the General."*

Chapter Fifty-One

Jim was sitting in the General Aviation passenger terminal when he saw what he thought was one of Black Water's Gulfstream jets pulling onto the ramp.

Grabbing his suitcase, he headed out the door just as the stairs came out of the plane, and a man wearing a white shirt with epaulets on the shoulders denoting him as the Captain came down.

"Mr. Lashley?" the guy said as Jim met him halfway across the ramp.

"Yes, sir," Jim said, extending his hand to shake.

"Hi," the Captain said, shaking Jim's hand. "I'm Randy, and I'm just running in to check the weather and make sure our flight plan is still good.

Go ahead and get on board," he continued. "Sammy, my co-pilot will put your suitcase on when he finishes the walk around."

"Nice to meet you, Randy," Jim said. "If it's all right with you, I'll just carry my suitcase up when I go."

"That's fine," Randy told him, nodding. "Just let Sammy know so he doesn't waste time looking for it."

Just as he was about to climb up the stairs, another guy came out of the doorway. "Hey," he said. "Just leave your bag, and I'll get it."

"I'll bring it up," Jim told him. "I just talked to Randy, and he said it's all right. You must be Sammy."

"Yes, sir. That's me," he replied, coming down the stairs. "Just toss your bag in the storage area as you get on unless you'll need it in flight."

"I'll do that," Jim told him. "I don't think I'll need anything before we get there."

"You might want to think about that," Sammy said, laughing. "It's my leg, and I'm still pretty new on this airplane. I've even scared the crap out of myself a couple of times."

"Understood," Jim said, heading up the stairs. "But I'll take my chances. I've flown with some pretty shaky pilots over the years, and I haven't soiled myself yet."

After setting his suitcase in the storage compartment just inside the door, Jim walked back to where Gene and two other guys were sitting.

"Good morning," Jim said as he got to their seats.

"About time," Gene joked, standing up to shake his hand. "I was worried that you'd decided you'd rather spend the day with a certain lovely young lady than come do what we're paying you for."

"Pay him no attention, guys," Jim said, smiling as he shook hands with Javier and Rob. "I'm sure you've been with the company long enough to know what a busybody the General can be."

"What? Me?" Gene complained as they took their seats. "When have I ever meddled in your personal life?"

"We won't have time to cover all of that before we get to Galveston," Jim said, laughing. "Let's just say that you've taken a keen interest in my welfare over the last few years."

For the next hour-and-a-half en route to the airport at Galveston, they avoided talking about the mission set for tomorrow in case they might be overheard by the pilots.

Once at the hotel, they met in Gene's room to review their plans and see if there had been any new information that might impact the operation.

After going over every detail for an hour, Gene decided that it was time to go have dinner and then meet again in the morning to see if there were any changes overnight to be considered.

Chapter Fifty-Two

"Okay," Gene told them as they were finishing their breakfast the next morning at Denny's. "I just learned that the new oyster boat will be ready to head out to sea this afternoon. We've informed the Coast Guard, and they'll board it before it leaves our territorial waters.

That will ensure that even if the boat from Mexico leaves with the fentanyl, it will never reach the states," Gene finished.

"That shouldn't have any impact on our plans," Jim said. "It might even help convince Jason and company that Javier arranged the meeting knowing the operation was about to begin today."

"How soon will you guys be ready to go?" Gene asked as he signaled for their check.

"I'd say give us an hour or so to get back to the hotel and do one more check of our equipment," Jim answered. "Has the company called to confirm the time with Jason?"

"No, we've decided to have Javier make the call this morning since he's the one taking the meeting," Gene explained. "So, when we get back to the hotel, Javier will call Jason and tell him what time for him, Maria, and Gilliad to be at the company.

We thought having him make the call would be better since they'll be hearing his voice when you get there," he continued. "Plus, it would be unreasonable for Ruben to make the call since he can't possibly know when Javier is ready to meet them."

"That is better," Jim agreed. "Since Jason knows Javier is coming, it would be most likely that he'd set the time after he gets here."

"One other thing," Gene said, handing the waiter his credit card. "We've been thinking about leaving one of the guns we picked up in Chicago when you leave the conference room."

"Why?" Jim asked. "Are you trying to tie their deaths to some gang up there?"

"At least muddy the water," Gene answered. "Do you have any reason not to leave one?"

Jim thought for a moment and then suggested, "If we're going to do that, it would look strange for a gun to be lying around if no shots were fired.

What if we stick it in the back of Jason's pants?" he continued. "I'm pretty sure if it was found on the floor, someone would think it had been planted."

"I've got an ankle holster," Javier suggested. "Why don't we put the gun in it and strap it to his ankle before we leave? That would be more believable."

"That's a good idea," Gene agreed. "But, let's get it scrubbed before you leave the hotel. We don't want any strange DNA showing up on it if they happen to run any tests.

We'll stop by and get some alcohol to wipe it down on the way back to the hotel," he finished as the waiter returned with the bill and his credit card.

"Let's get some hand lotion, too," Jim suggested. "We can smear a little on the holster to cover the smell of the alcohol, and since that will also rub off on Jason's ankle, it should avoid any suspicions."

"Good," Gene said, standing. "Let's get going, and maybe we can finish this before lunch."

"Has someone made sure that any cameras in the vicinity of the Oyster Company are inoperative?" Jim asked as they left the restaurant.

"Done," Gene answered, getting into the Suburban. "All of them within a two-block area will be disabled. Since it's Saturday, there shouldn't be anyone in the office except the people there for the meeting.

The folks from the lab or those on the production line don't have any reason to come in, but we've killed all of the cameras throughout the entire facility anyway," he finished.

"What do we do if someone comes in while we're there?" Rob asked.

"Leave them alone," Jim answered. "I don't want any innocent people hurt in this operation. The odds of someone seeing us are slim, and if I'm seen, the company has a fictitious record of who I am if they pick me out as having been there before.

If there are any exceptions to that rule, I'll be the one to make that decision," Jim finished as they headed back to the hotel. "The company will ensure you'll never be identified. The bottom line is if things go to shit, you guys walk out of the door and leave. I'll handle it from there. Understood?"

"Understood," Javier and Rob said in unison, nodding.

Chapter Fifty-Three

When they arrived back at the hotel, Gene said, "You guys go to your rooms and recheck everything. Javier, do whatever you need to do with the ankle holster and all of you meet me in my room in thirty minutes."

As they came into his room as he had requested, he was on the phone motioning for them to close the door, saying, "Okay, Valerie, they're all here. Are you ready to activate their phones?"

Hearing she was, he handed each of them a pair of tiny earbuds, telling Jim and the other two to listen for their names to be called.

"All right," everyone heard over their earbuds, "Your microphone will be hot from this moment on. My name is Valerie, and I'll be monitoring your mission today. And please just call me Val.

Let's start with a com check. Gene, if you'd please start and then work clockwise around the room," she directed.

"Gene," he said, then looking at Jim.

"Jim," Jim said, turning to look at Javier.

"Javier."

"Rob."

"Looks good from here," Val told them. "Now, let's do a location check. Starting again with Gene as a reference point, I'll call out your position in relation to him and then to each of you with your relative positions to the last person. Understood?

Jim, you're standing about five feet to Gene's left. Javier, you're ten feet to Jim's left, and Rob is eight feet to your left," she continued. "And Gene, you're fifteen feet to Rob's left. Is that correct?"

"Damn close," Gene told her, looking at where everyone was in the room.

"Good," she replied. "Now, we'll be following each of you from this moment until Gene terminates this operation. At that time, your phones will be deactivated, and you'll be on your own.

I have an operator dedicated to monitoring each of you," she explained. "Their job is to relay any information you need regarding the other agents or handle any potential problems from technical issues to threats.

We activated the phones of the people who are meeting you weeks ago," she continued. "We've been monitoring them since the DEA contacted Black Water and requested our assistance. At that time, the company inserted the same program into their phones that you have in yours.

I'll be able to pass on anything they say or what's picked up on their phones for approximately fifty feet around them, as well as their location in relation to where any of you are at that moment," she finished. "Now, if there are no questions, I'll leave you guys until Gene lets me know the operation is terminated."

"Time for your call, Javier," Gene told him after thanking Val and motioning at the phone in his room. "Let's get this started."

As the phone was answered, Javier said, "Good morning, Jason. This is Javier Guzman. I believe Ruben told you to expect me today and that you'll have arranged for me to meet you, Maria, and Michael Gilliad. Are they there?"

Nodding, Javier continued, "I will be there in forty-five minutes. Please have someone meet me at the entrance and escort me to where we'll be meeting."

Listening for a moment, he said, "Mr. Strong, I understand your concerns. But, if you have any comments or questions regarding my reasons for being here or my authority, I suggest you call El Disenos and resolve any issues with him before I arrive. Is that clear?

Excellent," Javier said, nodding and looking at the others in the room. "I'll be there now in forty-three minutes. And if it isn't already obvious, I will not look favorably if I discover that any of you have a weapon of any kind.

I'm not here to cause any problems," he continued. "But if threatened, I will most assuredly terminate the meeting as well as the person making the threat. So, I think it would be in your interest, as well as your friends there, to make this as quick and painless as possible.

So, let's just get it over with, and I can report back to Ruben that we're all on the same page regarding restoring our operation to its full capacity until we've made up for the unfortunate losses we've incurred," Javier said.

"What do you think?" he asked Gene after hanging up the phone.

"Good," Gene answered. "Now, I have neoprene gloves for each of you. Once you're ready to leave the Oyster Company, put on your gloves and wipe down anything you've touched, especially in the conference room.

Javier, have you handled the magazine in the gun you're leaving on Jason?" Gene asked then said, "Doesn't matter, wipe it down now and make sure you don't touch it again.

It should go without saying, but please limit what you do touch to as little as possible," Gene instructed. "Treat this as you would any other mission. Leave nothing connecting the company or you to the scene."

Taking a small box from his briefcase lying on the bed, Gene handed it to Jim, saying, "Here are the three nasal sprays for your targets. Just put them back in the box when you've used them. And please … be careful. I don't want to leave four dead bodies in that room.

There are also three nasal sprays of Naloxone, the antidote for fentanyl overdose if you need them," he added. "They're the ones with the green stripe.

Now, if there's nothing else," Gene finished as Jim looked into the box, "Let's go meet the pre-deceased."

Chapter Fifty-Four

After dropping off Gene and Jim a couple of blocks from the Oyster Company, Rob drove to the front of the building and stopped at the sidewalk leading to the doors.

Getting out, he followed Javier toward the entrance, which opened as they got several feet from it.

"Mr. Guzman," Jason said, coming down to greet them. "Welcome to Galveston."

"Jason," Javier said, shaking his hand. "Good to meet you. This is my assistant, Roberto. He'll be accompanying me to our meeting."

Looking at Rob, Jason complained, "I wasn't told that anyone other than you would be attending."

"Then I guess I'm telling you now," Javier said, staring at Jason. "As I've already told you, if you have any questions regarding me or my authority, you have the number to call. Do we have a problem already?"

Jason quickly responded, "No. No. Not at all. It's just that I …"

"Good," Javier cut him off. "Now, would you please take me to meet the others?"

Listening to the conversation, Gene and Jim waited until they heard that Javier and Rob were in the conference room before walking over. When they arrived at the Oyster Company headquarters, Gene got in the Suburban and told Jim, "I'll park over beside the other cars and come back to get you when you're ready to come out. I don't want anyone to see the car sitting here and start wondering what's happening.

I'll stay in the car and monitor your progress," he continued as he got into the driver's seat. "If you think you need my assistance, just let me know."

"I don't think that will be necessary," Jim said as he listened to Javier and Rob being introduced to Maria and Michael. "I'm going to give them another ten minutes or so, and then I'll join them."

As Gene was driving away, Jim stepped into the lobby, carefully checking to see if there was anyone unexpected around as he heard Javier say, "Ruben tells me that you have the capacity to increase production by fifty percent. Is that correct?"

"Yes, sir," Jason said. "I can have the extra workers here when our boat returns."

"Then you must actually have the capacity to increase production by one hundred percent," Javier said, leaning forward and looking directly at Jason.

"Impossible," Jason almost screamed. "You know nothing about my operation's capabilities, and you're demanding that I increase by twice what we're capable of doing?"

"You will increase your production as I have said," Javier said, leaning back and steepling his fingers against his chest. "That topic is not up for negotiation."

Leaning forward again, he continued, "And not only will you increase the output as Ruben has demanded, but you will also continue that level indefinitely."

"Bullshit," Jason shouted, shaking his head. "First, we simply can't ramp up our production at the snap of your fingers. And there's no need to sustain that level of production past the point that we've replaced the lost product.

And why would we double our production anyway," Jason argued. "We can't possibly distribute that much product. We don't have enough dealers to handle it."

"I'll be handling the increase," Javier said, smiling. "We've opened a new market with its hub in Chicago. I'll be performing the same as Michael as far as street distribution. You'll have nothing to do with my operation other than supplying me with the product I require.

Now, if you're unable to meet our demands, we'll simply replace you," Javier told him, leaning back again.

"I'll call Ruben myself," Maria suddenly said. "This is my family. Ruben is my family. You can't come in here and make demands and threats that you'll replace my husband and me or take over our operation."

Javier took his phone out and slid it across the table to Maria, saying, "Here, use my phone. His number is number one on speed dial."

Knowing that Black Water had Ruben's phone blocked and was standing by for the anticipated call from anyone at the meeting, he sat back and stared at Maria as she made the call.

"Ruben," she finally said. "Just who is this *bastardo* you've sent us? He's making impossible demands and has threatened my husband and me with being removed from the business we've built for you."

Listening for a second, she continued, "No. That's not going to happen. *We* run this company. All you do is sit over there, spending the money *we* send you. This is just not fair."

Listening again for several moments, she finally handed the phone to Javier and said, "He wants to talk to you."

Chapter Fifty-Five

Javier was agreeing with the fictitious Ruben on the phone when Jim opened the door to the conference room. As Jason, Maria, and Michael turned to see who had entered, Javier put the phone on the table and pulled his pistol from the back of his pants.

"North, what are you doing back here?" Jason asked as Jim stepped into the room and headed for the end of the table where they were sitting.

"I've returned to deliver a message," Jim said as they saw Javier and Rob pointing their guns at them.

"For now, do not get out of your chairs. Place your arms on the armrests and keep your feet beneath the chair," Jim ordered as he set the box containing the fentanyl nasal sprays on the table and pulled a package of long, heavy Zip ties from one of his back pockets.

"Javier, you and Rob shoot anyone in the shoulder who makes the slightest move to get out of their chair," Jim said, walking back behind Jason's chair.

As he pulled the chair away from the table, he continued, "If they move a second time, shoot them in the face."

Stepping between Jason and the table, Jim used two Zip ties to secure Jason's wrists to the arms of the chair. Then, bending down, he pulled Jason's feet forward, and Zip tied his ankles to the legs of the chair.

Stepping behind Maria's chair, he repeated the process and then moved to Michael's chair to finish securing the three of them in their chairs.

Finished, Jim returned to the head of the table and opened the box he had put down before tying them to their chairs.

"This," Jim said, removing one of the nasal sprays, "is five milligrams of fentanyl. *Five* milligrams."

Taking the other two out of the box and setting them on the table, he continued, "I've brought one of these special nasal sprays for each of you. So don't get concerned that you're being left out of this morning's little drug experiment.

Now I'm sure you know just how powerful and dangerous this little synthetic opioid that you've been bringing in from Mexico is," Jim said, looking at each and lightly shaking the nasal spray he held.

"But I'm going to refresh your memory, just in case you've forgotten what you're doing to thousands of people just so you can have a bigger house, a newer car, or, in the case of Jason, another mistress up in Texas City," he continued.

Looking at Maria, he asked, "What? You didn't know about her? Sweet little twenty-two-year-old with beautiful long blond hair and the nicest sets of enhanced breasts I've ever seen. Your husband is such a nice guy. Pays for a very nice apartment. Brand new Lexus. Plus, a very, *very* generous allowance. A true philanthropist. Jason, Jason, Jason," he said, turning to look at him and shaking his head. "How could you do that to your sweet wife?

I mean, just because she's been banging Michael there while you're here putting fentanyl in the little oyster shells doesn't make it right for you to be screwing your private little Barbie Doll," Jim said, looking at the three of them. "You know that old Chinese saying, "Two Wongs don't make a Wyatt.

Okay, back to refreshing your memories," Jim said, letting them get a closer look at the sprayer. "Fentanyl, like other opioids, attaches itself to the endorphin-releasing receptors in the brain.

More specifically, the receptors that tell the brain it's running out of oxygen or that the carbon dioxide level is too high," he continued.

"By blocking those receptors, the brain will not tell the lungs to take a breath. And that's a fairly important function of the lungs. Breathing," he added.

"Now, since the brain doesn't tell the lungs what to do, the oxygen levels continue to decrease, and the brain slowly dies," Jim told them, setting one of the sprays in front of each of them.

"It usually only takes two milligrams of fentanyl to cause this to happen unless you're very large or have developed a higher resistance due to repeated use," he continued.

"Since I don't think any of you have been using this nasty little concoction, and none of you are much above average, even though Maria says Michael is *WAY* above average," Jim said, looking at Jason. "Although it could be she only means compared to you.

I only mention that because your little Barbie Doll has a Ken Doll over as soon as you leave," Jim said, smiling at him. "Guess you aren't satisfying either one of them.

Now I'm pretty sure the *five* milligrams in each of these little devices will have you entering the first stages of hypoxia about three minutes after I administer these *five* milligrams," Jim said, looking from face to face. "And I intend on making sure you get all that's coming to you. Every frigging milligram down to the last droplet.

That means you're about to die," Jim whispered loudly.

"Now, this is Naloxone," Jim told them, holding up one of the other nasal sprays from the box. "It's the only known antidote for opioid overdoses. I've brought three.

Now, I'll tell you that once I administer the Naloxone, if I do, you'll have about thirty minutes to get to a hospital and receive treatment, or the Naloxone will lose its effectiveness, and the fentanyl will bump it off the receptor, and the process will begin again," Jim said looking at each of them.

Rob, would you please step around behind Mr. Strong and hold his head steady while I send him to join all those he's caused to suffer the same horrid death?" Jim said, holding the spray in his right hand and pushing Jason back in the chair with his left.

Chapter Fifty-Six

"Wait! Wait!" Maria cried. "You don't have to do this. I can give you the names of all of Ruben's people who are involved with moving the fentanyl across the border into every state from Texas to California!"

"I can do better than that. I can give you the names of all of my distributors," Michael quickly shouted. "That will lead you to every distributor and street dealer in every city where we've been doing business."

Then Jason chimed in, saying, "I can do better than any of them. I can make each of you rich. Richer than you can imagine. I've been taking a pound out of each hundred pounds we ship for years and selling it to another guy who's not involved with Michael.

I've got millions. Hundreds of millions! It's all in safety deposit boxes across Texas," he continued. "It's yours if you'll just let me go."

"Somehow, I don't think any of you are telling me the truth," Jim finally said as Rob stepped behind Jason. "Or at least not all of it. Rob, hold his head."

As Rob grabbed Jason's ears and held his head, Jim shoved the sprayer up his nose and emptied it, saying, "Now, Maria."

As Rob held her hair to keep her motionless, Jim repeated the process and emptied the sprayer into her nose as she tried desperately to avoid it.

Nodding at Rob, Jim took the last spray from the table and shoved Michael back into his chair as Rob grabbed his ears.

"Now, if anybody has anything to add, now is your last chance," Jim told them, walking back to where he had left the Naloxone. "You have three minutes at the most before your brain begins to suffer permanent damage.

Around four minutes, you'll probably go into a coma, from which you might never recover," he continued as he waved a bottle of the Naloxone sprays in front of them. "Now is your last chance to tell me exactly what you said you would tell me just a moment ago."

For the next couple of minutes, each of them shouted every name or piece of information they could possibly do in the short time they had left.

When they finally stopped talking, Jim simply put the Naloxene back in the box as each of them began to shout that they had kept their promise to tell him everything they knew and demanded they get the antidote.

Jim paused, smiling at them, and then said, "Maybe you should have listened better. I never said I wouldn't administer the exact form of death that you have spread across the country.

Nor did I promise to give you the antidote if you told me everything you knew," he continued watching them. "Now, I'm going to have a seat across from you and watch as death descends upon each of you, and your soul is snatched by the devil himself."

A few moments later, when the three had finally ceased all movement, Jim told Javier and Rob to cut the Zip ties and put them in their pockets.

Putting on his neoprene gloves, he took some Handi Wipes from his pocket and said, "Okay, guys, let's wrap this up. Put your gloves on and start wiping everything down you may have touched. Javier put the ankle holster and gun on Jason's right ankle. Don't forget to put Jason's prints on the gun before you put it in the holster."

As he watched the guys work, he said, "Gene, we'll be out of here in five minutes. I hope the folks at Black Water got all of the information. These people got rather chatty toward the end."

"We got it all. Every last word," he heard Val saying. "It'll take us a day or two to get the information out. But I'd say the DEA and other folks will have their work cut out for them for weeks to come."

"Just double-check everything before you come out," Gene told them. "Don't forget the door handles as you leave, either. I'll be waiting at the curb when you're done. Val, deactivate their phones. We're done here."

Chapter Fifty-Seven

A couple of hours later, after they had checked out of the hotel and boarded the company Gulfstream to take them home, Gene looked at Jim and the others, saying, "That was a good operation, guys. I got a call from the company saying that the DEA is most grateful.

The operation down in Mexico has been accelerated since the assassination of El Disenos and a couple of his close associates," he continued, nodding at each of them. "And the Border Patrol now has the names and pictures of the people Maria provided.

All together, it was definitely a success," he finished.

"I'm surprised you got close enough to El Disenos to take him out," Jim replied. "I mean, the guy must have some of the tightest security imaginable to survive all of the rivals to his drug empire."

"I'll admit it took months of planning and not just a little luck," Gene admitted. "The company, on behalf of the DEA and the US Border Patrol, has had him under close scrutiny for a long time.

We analyzed every movement, every aspect of his life, every opportunity when his security was the weakest," he continued.

"It finally came down to when he met his mistress," Gene told them. "Ruben had provided her with an apartment in one of the tallest buildings in Acapulco. Matter of fact, her apartment covered the entire top floor.

Ruben would fly one of his jets to Acapulco and then have his helicopter take him to a landing pad on top of the building," Gene said, smiling. "He had a small but effective security team that kept watch of the lady and would give final clearance to land once they had made sure there was no threat at the building since they controlled access to the roof.

I guess they got a little sloppy with their perimeter," he told them. "At least they didn't consider anything outside of a block a threat. That was their fatal mistake.

We just happened to have one of the finest snipers in the world in our organization. A fellow named Knox," Gene explained. "He doesn't hold any records like the Canadian Rob Furlong, whose best shot is a little over 2,600 yards. That's just under a mile and a half!

The famous Carlos Hancock is in the same category with a kill at 2,500 yards," he added. "Now, our guy may not hold any records or be as well known, but he's certainly good enough to reach out and touch you if you're within a mile.

One mile, 1,760 yards. Five thousand two hundred and eighty feet," Gene told them. "After the company saw the perimeter of Ruben's security at Acapulco, which was just over a half mile, they gained access to a building one story taller than where his mistress lived just outside the zone his people thought would afford them protection from any threat.

Ruben's security team finally convinced him that he was under attack after the two boats went down and that he might not be safe staying in Mexico City," Gene said. "When he left his residence, we waited to see where he would go.

As soon as we learned about his flight plan to Acapulco, we alerted Knox and his team to expect him within the next couple of hours and to be prepared to take the shot," he said.

"Since we knew his arrival time at the airport and a close estimate of when he'd land on the building where his love interest was … Knox was just waiting for him to step to the door of the helicopter," Gene told them. "With his security team standing on the roof, Ruben would be about three feet above them, standing in the open door.

The shot was pretty simple. We knew exactly where the helicopter would sit down since there's a big red circle with an 'H' painted inside," Gene continued. "But the window of opportunity was mere seconds.

We had small Mexican flags on several buildings between Knox and that building, as well as an anemometer installed on a corner of his roof," he explained. "So, our guy had every variable he needed to know to make the shot.

As the door to the Huey slid open and Ruben was about to step down, Knox pulled the trigger on the Barrett M82 he was using and put a fifty-caliber round through his chest," Gene finished. "As the round knocked him back into the helicopter, Knox fired a second round that he says most likely struck Ruben in the genitals."

"Damn," Javier and Rob said in unison, grabbing their crotches. "Even if you're dead, that's got to hurt."

"At least Knox shot him in the chest before shooting his nuts off," Jim said, laughing. "It could have been the other way around."

Chapter Fifty-Eight

After landing back at Love Field, Gene followed Jim to the terminal as the plane was being refueled, and the Captain checked the weather in Chicago.

"So, what are you going to do with the couple of days you have off?" Gene asked.

"Not sure yet," Jim answered, setting his suitcase down. "I'm supposed to go look at Marie's house. I think she said the guys remodeling it are almost finished, and she wanted to see how it was going."

"Speaking of Marie," Gene interrupted. "Please tell her I said 'Hi'."

"Sure," Jim said, looking quizzically at Gene. "Is there something else?"

"Yes, sorry, I jumped in," Gene apologized. "What I wanted to tell you was that the CIA's man in the Aryan Circle has made contact with the guy who shot her husband.

Bob was given the name of a little biker bar where Jack likes to hang out," Gene continued. "It's frequented by a lot of the wannabes, like Jack.

When we learned about that, we arranged for one of our people to get a job there tending bar," Gene added. "And we had a couple of our ladies start showing up there occasionally."

"That's pretty damn risky to be sending females into that environment, isn't it?" Jim asked, surprised that the company would approve.

"Not really," Gene said, laughing. "We had one rather huge gentleman come in with them the first time they went. And I mean huge. And a shit load of tattoos. The man is six feet and eight inches tall and weighs about three hundred pounds, and not an ounce of flab.

Anyway, he sat down with the girls and waited for the inevitable testosterone levels to peak," he continued, trying not to laugh again. "Then he goes to the bathroom, and when he comes back, some 'tough guy' is standing by his chair, leaning over and making what I'd consider to be rather rude comments.

Our guy walks up behind him, grabs him by the neck of his leather vest and the top of his pants," he said, grinning and shaking his head. "He picked the guy up like a cat picks up a mouse. He literally tosses the guy about three feet.

He then steps over to him as he's lying on the floor and says, "*If anyone of you motherfuckers even looks at my sister or her friend again, I'll rip your fucking head off and shit down your throat.*"

"I guess that sort of got everyone's attention," Jim said, visualizing the scene.

"Without a doubt," Gene replied. "Suddenly, every guy in the place developed an interest in the top of their tables."

"I can imagine," Jim said, shaking his head. "Did that end it?"

"Oh yes," Gene answered. "And, we had them come in again with Bob the first time he went. Between his Aryan

Circle tattoos showing, and being with the sister of the biggest man they've ever seen, not a soul even looked their way.

One guy, who must not have been there the first time, turned to look at one of the ladies as she was walking by him going to the lady's room," Gen added. "Bob simply walked over and asked, '*Interested, asshole?*'

Another guy at the table jumped in saying, '*No. Not at all. He just thought she looked like one of the waitresses at the IHOP where we had breakfast this morning. Isn't that right?*'" Gene said, not able to contain his laughter. "As the guy was staring a hole through the guy who was watching, he finally figured out that he better agree and just apologize.

'*I'm sorry, mister,*'" he said. '*I didn't mean any disrespect.*'" Gene finished. "There hasn't been anyone even looking at them since then. Word spread like wildfire through that group and all of their friends."

"And now that leads us to … ?" Jim asked as the Captain waved on his way back to the plane.

"So our bartender let Bob know when Jack was there," Gene answered. "He picks up the ladies and heads over.

Spotting Jack as he walks in, he nods and takes a table across the room." he continued.

"Jack must have thought that Bob had shown respect and might be approachable. So he waits until Bob and the girls have their beers, walks over, and tells them their next beers are on him," Gene said.

"Bob merely looks at him like you'd look at a bug and says, '*No, you won't. I don't know you.*'" he continued. "Then Jack tells him about people he knows within the Aryan Circle, how he believes in their mission, and then blathers on about how he'd like to be a member.

Bob gives him another quick look of disgust and turns back to the girls saying, '*Don't count on it,* '" Gene finished. "We're waiting for the next time we can get them together and have Bob make a small gesture to encourage Jack to fall into our plan when we offer him a chance to shoot another police officer."

"So when do you think we can set it up?" Jim asked.

"Probably won't happen until you get back from your next trip," Gene answered. "We'd like to have a couple more times where Jack sees Bob. We think he'll be even more eager since he thinks he knows Bob. Let's not rush this. He'd probably take the bait right now, but we're also waiting for our guy with the Dallas Police Department to make some of the arrangements."

"Okay," Jim said, shaking Gene's hand, knowing they needed to get Javier and Rob to Chicago. "Just keep me in the loop."

"You know I will," Gene said as he turned to go back to the plane. "And don't forget to tell Marie 'Hi' for me."

Chapter Fifty-Nine

When Jim got home, the first thing he wanted to do was take a long shower. Tossing his suitcase on the bed, he quickly stripped and put the clothes he had worn since this morning in the hamper in the master bath.

After scrubbing the events of the morning from his body, he gave up trying to scrub his mind clean. Thinking about the harm those three people had done to countless thousands would remain with him through more showers than he had time for.

Walking into the living room with just the towel around his waist, he turned on the TV to catch the local news before calling Marie to let her know he was home.

As WFAA Channel 8 appeared on the screen, Jim saw a scene obviously from the Galveston Gulf Coast Oyster Company's parking lot. "*Damn, that was fast*," he thought as he tried to shake some water from his left ear.

As the reporter from KHOU was speaking to the camera about the three bodies that had been discovered less than an hour ago by one of the lab assistants who had come in to get some notes he had forgotten when he left the day before, Jim thought about what would have happened if the guy had stopped by a couple of hours earlier.

"At least I don't have that on my conscious," he said aloud as he sat down on the couch to see what, if any, information they had about the event.

Finally, after an officer from the Galveston Police Department gave a quick statement about not commenting on an ongoing investigation, Jim headed back to the bathroom to get ready to see Marie.

Twenty minutes later, now dressed in freshly starched Wranglers and a white button-down collar shirt, he dialed her number while he rooted around the refrigerator for a beer.

"Hey," he said when she answered. "Is the offer to see your house still open?"

Hearing it was, he asked, "Do you want me to come to your dad's house and get you or should I just meet you at yours?

That works for me," Jim said when she told him to come to hers. "Just give me the address, and I'll be there as quick as the speed limit allows.

Okay, I'll see you there," he said before hanging up.

Finishing his beer, he took a quick look at the map and found the address she had given him. Looked like it was about halfway to where her mom and dad lived. Scribbling some notes of the streets to take, he grabbed his keys from the table and headed out the door.

Heading north on 635, he quickly came to the exit for Ferguson Road and then took the access road until reaching South Garland Ave and made a right turn.

A couple of miles later, he came to West Miller Road and turned left, now keeping his eye out for Morningside Drive.

Almost a mile later, he spotted it and turned right, looking at the house numbers painted on the curb. From the number of the first house he saw on the left, it appeared he had about nine houses before reaching Marie's.

Spotting it, he parked across the street and walked up the driveway past two pickups with ladders and paint cans in the beds. Reaching the door, he pressed the doorbell and waited.

Moments later, the door opened and Marie said, "Jim, good to see you. Come in. Did you have any trouble finding me?"

"No problem," Jim said, looking around at the obviously recently painted walls. "And I like the tan color in this room. Living room, I'm guessing."

"Yes, let me show you the rest of the house," she confirmed, taking his hand.

For the next hour, she led him from room to room, telling him what it had looked like before remodeling and what was left to do. When they finally finished the tour, she asked, "What do you think?"

"Looks good," he answered, nodding. "I really like how you've taken out the wall between the kitchen and the dining room. Having just the counter between the rooms makes it easy to set everything on the counter and then put it on the table when you're ready."

"Even better, when I clear the table, I just set everything on the counter, and it's in reach from the sink or the dishwasher," she commented.

"Nice," Jim told her, looking around at the bare walls. "I'm sure you'll be glad when you can hang pictures or whatever decorations you'll be putting back in the rooms."

"Yeah, it's been too long since I've felt at home here," she replied, looking around. "I waited too long to start this.

This was our house, David's and mine. At first, I couldn't bear to think about changing anything.

You know," she said, looking at Jim. "It was like destroying memories."

"I know what you mean," Jim said, putting his arms around her. "But I finally realized that memories are in my head. Oh, I still have a memento or two around. But Jennifer doesn't live there anymore. I do."

Chapter Sixty

After the tour, Jim followed Marie to the restaurant and parked beside her. As he got out of the pickup, she took his hand and said, "Dad said he'll make some time to come sit with us after we eat. I'm not sure what he's preparing, but he told me we wouldn't need the menu."

"Lasagna," Jim said, smiling as they came to the door. "That's my bet."

"I'll take that bet," Marie said as they entered. "How much?"

"Two dollars," Jim answered as Aurora met them at the door.

"What's two dollars?" she asked as Marie kissed her cheek.

"A bet on what Dad is making us for dinner, Mom," Marie answered.

"Oh?" Aurora said, looking from her to Jim. "And what did you pick, Jim?"

"Lasagna," Jim told her. "I figured since he likes to tease me about it because of my first time here, I figured he'd want to rub it in."

"Well then, I want a two-dollar bet also," she replied.

"Oh, no," Marie told her. "You know what Dad's cooking, so that wouldn't be fair."

"I don't care about fair," Aurora said, laughing. "I just want to win the bet."

"I'll do this," Jim said, putting his hand on Aurora's shoulder. "I'll let you bet two dollars on Marie's guess. Now, that's fair."

"Oh, pooh," Aurora said, shaking her head. "She doesn't know. Why should I chance losing two dollars when I know what it is?"

Marie leaned over and whispered in Aurora's ear. Aurora suddenly smiled and said, "I've changed my mind. I'll bet two dollars on what Marie picks!"

"So that's the way it is," Jim exclaimed. "I'm being set up by you two. Marie obviously knows, and suddenly, you want to bet with her? Nope, bet's off."

"What bet's off?" Anthony asked, coming from the kitchen and wiping his hands on his apron.

"Jim bet two dollars on what you're making for our dinner tonight," Marie explained. "He already picked Lasagna, and Mom and I are going to pick something else."

"Okay," Anthony said as he leaned to whisper in Jim's ear. "Now, it's an even bet."

"No, he picked Lasagna," Marie argued. "He can't change!"

Anthony thought for a second and then said, "Fine. Now you make your bet."

"I'm betting Lobster Ravioli," Marie said, smiling.

"And you, my devious little darling wife, what's your bet?" he asked.

"I'm with my beautiful daughter, Marie," Aurora said, crossing her arms.

"Then you take them back to their table," Anthony said, looking at her. "Then come get that bottle of Castello Banfi Brunello Di Montalcino I've been saving.

And put two extra glasses on the table for when we toast the winner of this two-dollar bet," he finished, turning to return to the kitchen.

"So, what did Dad say to you?" Marie asked as Aurora headed back to the front of the restaurant.

"I can't tell you what your father told me in the strictest of confidence," Jim said, smiling.

"He told you what he's making, didn't he?" she asked, slapping his arm. "That's not fair."

"Fair?" Jim asked incredulously. "You already knew, your mother already knew, and you conspired to take the last two dollars I have, and I'll need for lunch tomorrow, and you tell me I'm not being fair?"

"I still want to know," she repeated as Aurora came back with a bottle of wine and four glasses.

"Know what?" Aurora asked, pouring a little wine in two of the glasses.

"What Dad said to him," Marie answered.

"It doesn't matter," Aurora said. "He's made his pick … and we picked Lobster Ravioli."

"That's right, Mr. Smartypants. You're stuck with lasagna," Marie said, sticking her tongue out at him.

As Jim shook his head and picked up his glass, Anthony came in with a covered tray balanced on his right hand, saying, "I hope you're ready because here's the first course of your evening meal."

Setting the tray on the edge of the table, he whipped off the white cloth that covered the tray and said, "Lasagna. Fresh from the refrigerator! Bon appetite."

Chapter Sixty-One

Fifteen minutes later, Aurora came back to their table with a tray with two Caesar salads and two plates of Lobster Ravioli. As she set them in front of Jim and Marie, she said, "Marie, your father says he hopes both of you enjoy the *second* course of this evening's meal … his words, not mine."

"It seems your father is more than just a Chef," Jim said as Aurora placed his salad in front of him. "Not to bring up a biblical reference, but he displayed the wisdom of Solomon.

No, he didn't cut a baby in half. But he did award half of the meal to each of us," Jim continued. "You are most fortunate to have such a wise and fair man for your father. And as your husband, Aurora. Most fortunate."

"Oh, bite me," Marie said, laughing. "You men always stick together, especially when one of you is wrong."

"Wrong? *I* was wrong?" Jim asked as Aurora tried not to laugh. "Who conspired to cheat me?

I did nothing wrong," Jim said, looking innocently at Marie. "I even kept my choice of bet even after your dad told me the real answer. But you two. You did what we call '*insider trading.*' People have spent years in prison for such behavior."

"Let me see if I can rephrase this another way … bite me!" Marie said, throwing her napkin across the table at Jim. "You still owe me and mother two dollars."

"Fine," Jim said. "And each of you owes me two dollars. So, I'll pay you when you pay me."

"Back to the two-dollar bet, are you?" Anthony said, coming to their table. "As the head of this family, I declare all wagers null and void.

Now, my dear wife, if you'd be so kind as to pour two glasses of wine and join me while I enjoy a few minutes with my beautiful young daughter and a most interesting gentleman," he said, taking a seat.

As Aurora sat, Anthony took his glass and raised it, saying, "To family and friends. May they always be cherished!"

"To family and friends," the others parroted as they raised their glasses.

Setting his glass down, Anthony said, "Jim, Marie said you were down in Galveston working with some oyster company about security, I believe."

"That's correct," Jim answered.

"I just saw something this afternoon about some people who ran an oyster company being found dead in their office," Anthony continued. "I hope that wasn't the company you were working with."

"I believe that was the Galveston Gulf Coast Oyster Company," Jim said. "They didn't ask us to look into their security.

We looked into some things at the Fresh Bay Oyster Company," he continued, knowing he had shaded the truth.

"It's one of the smaller companies in the oyster business down there."

"That's good," Anthony replied, nodding. "Being associated with something like that is never good. Bad for business."

"I agree," Jim said. "Have they figured out what happened?"

"I don't believe so," Anthony answered. "At least they aren't telling the public."

"I don't want to know," Aurora said, taking a sip of her wine. "I have enough to worry about up here. Two grandchildren I don't get to see often enough.

And incompetent law that can't manage to find the man who killed my son-in-law. Why should I worry about things that don't affect me?" she finished.

"Things like that affect all of us," Anthony argued. "Just like up here. People die, and no one is held responsible. I, myself, hope they find out who killed those folks. Just as I hope they find the man who killed David.

Anyway, enough of that," Anthony concluded, shaking his head. "Let's move to something not so depressing. This is an evening to enjoy."

"I agree," Jim said, raising his glass to Tony. "And I have to say that I've enjoyed getting to know you. All of you."

"Thank you," Aurora said, raising her glass. "And we've enjoyed getting to know you. I think Marie's very lucky to meet someone like you."

"Mom," Marie said with a look that was meant to convey 'shut up,' "I think we're all lucky that Jim picked our restaurant to visit."

"That we are," Anthony said, raising his glass. "The world has a way of setting things right if we just have patience."

After taking a drink of his wine, Anthony asked, "What are you going to do now, Jim? Some more travel?"

"I guess you can call it travel," Jim answered. "I've got to go fly again tomorrow afternoon. Except this is for American, not for fun."

"Isn't it fun to fly those big airplanes?" Aurora asked. "I've always wondered what it would be like." "It's like driving a big bus that has a hundred and fifty unhappy strangers sitting very closely beside each other," Jim told her, laughing. "And, not only are they sitting very close to each other, but they also have to crawl over each other to go to the bathroom, which they all seem to need to do ten minutes after takeoff. And every ten minutes after that."

Chapter Sixty-Two

After finishing their dinner, Anthony returned to the kitchen, and as Aurora carried the empty wine bottle away, Marie asked, "What are your plans for the rest of the evening?"

"Nothing, I guess," Jim answered. "Go home and pack my suitcase … again."

"What if I grab a movie and another bottle of wine," she suggested. "Think you can squeeze me in between packing your suitcase and needing to get the mandatory eight hours of *uninterrupted* rest?"

"That can probably be arranged," Jim answered, smiling. "But since I have to get up at four in the morning, that means I have to be in bed by eight tonight. It's already almost six, so I've got to be in bed in about two hours."

"Then I suggest we don't waste those two hours," Marie said as she got up. "I'll go to Mom's house and grab a couple of things and meet you at your house."

"Then I guess I better go thank your mom and dad," Jim said, getting up. "I hope they'll let me pay for dinner tonight. And I'm sure that bottle of wine costs more than I normally spend on a case."

"No, Dad would be terribly insulted if you even suggest paying," Marie told him. "He's been hoping that I find someone to be with for the last year or so. And Mom told me he's happy I've brought you into the family. Even if it's just as a friend, he misses David almost as much as I do, and I think he sees you as someone he would welcome into our family."

"I certainly don't want to insult your father," Jim replied. "But I can't keep accepting free dinners and expensive wine every time I come here."

"I'll talk to Mom," Marie said, holding Jim's hand as she headed for the door. "But for now, just thank him. I'll see you at your house."

Saying goodbye and heading for the door to the kitchen, Jim almost ran into Aurora as she was carrying out a tray for another diner. "Oops," Jim said, stepping out of her way. "I just wanted to say thanks to Anthony." "Go on in," she said, nodding. "I'll be right back as soon as I deliver this."

Stepping into the kitchen, Jim's nose was assaulted with the fragrances of the spices and herbs that permeated the air. Combined with the high humidity, it was almost overwhelming.

Seeing Jim, Anthony said something to one of the men working behind the stainless table where bowls of different ingredients for the dishes they were preparing sat.

Wiping his hands on his apron, he said, "I guess we evened out the score on that little bet, didn't we?" "Yes, we did," Jim said, nodding as he smiled. "I must say, that was a stroke of genius bringing out that almost frozen Lasagna."

Laughing loudly, he replied, "We men can't let women get the best of us all of the time. Now, sometimes we must submit, but I'm a true believer in balance in life."

"I'd say you balanced that just right," Jim said as Anthony put his hand on his shoulder. "But knowing women, we can expect retaliation sooner or later."

"The eternal dance," Anthony said with a slight smile. "It's what puts the spice in a relationship. If all you ever got was garlic, you'd yearn for oregano. And vice versa. Balance."

"I agree," Jim said. "I couldn't stand to spend my life with a woman who felt she had to agree with everything I said. Or did."

"That's what makes my Aurora such a treasure," Anthony agreed. "Oh, she says she's supporting everything I say or plan. But those little subtleties say different."

"Oh, yeah," Jim said, nodding. "My wife Jennifer was a master at that. Before long, I was agreeing with her, and she made me think it was my idea all along. And she was usually right."

"I think a wise woman will see the wisdom in letting her man believe he's got the final word," Anthony said, leading Jim from the kitchen. "Only a foolish woman would make him feel even slightly impotent."

"Balance," Jim said, shaking his hand. "And I do appreciate your hospitality and generosity. But ..."

"I understand," Anthony said, shushing Jim with his upheld hand. "A man, an honest and honorable man, cannot accept a gift without repayment.

One of these days, not so far in the future, I hope, perhaps you will invite my family to your place for what Marie said was a perfectly prepared mesquite grilled steak," he finished as they walked to the exit. "Until then, please allow a father to treat his favorite daughter and her friend to the occasional meal."

"With pleasure," Jim said, shaking Anthony's hand. "And when you and Aurora come, please, allow me to be as good a host as you've been.

And I'll make sure the girls have the night off so they can come as well," he finished as they stepped outside. "Allow me to thank all of you for supporting Marie. And welcoming me into the family circle. I enjoy having a family to spend time with. Even if they aren't my family."

"Did Jim already leave?" Aurora said as Anthony came back in.

"Yes, he just left," Anthony answered. "A good man. I hope Marie realizes what a good man he is."

"If you were half as observant as you think you are, you'd already know the answer to that," Aurora said, patting his cheek.

Chapter Sixty-Three

Three days later, after returning from his trip, Jim had barely gotten in his pickup when his phone rang. Answering "Hello" as he tossed his suitcase in the rear seat, he waited to see who was calling.

"Jim," Gene said. "How about I meet you at the house with a guest?"

"Sounds good," Jim answered. "Who's the guest?"

"Bob," Gene told him. "It's time you meet him, and we start working on the plan."

"Fine," Jim said, starting the pickup. "I'll be there in about an hour."

"Great," Gene replied. "See you then."

Driving home, Jim started wondering if something had come up and they needed to accelerate their planning regarding Robertson.

After maneuvering through the traffic between DFW and Mesquite, he pulled onto the street leading to his house and saw the familiar black Suburban sitting at the curb.

Parking in the driveway, he got out and grabbed his suitcase as Gene and a heavily tattooed man climbed out of the Suburban. "Gene, always a pleasure," Jim said as they met on the driveway and shook hands. "You guys come on in the house."

"Jim, this is Bob," Gene said as they started up the sidewalk. "Bob, Jim."

Jim turned to shake his hand and said, "Good to meet you, Bob."

"Likewise," Bob said as Jim turned to unlock the door. "You don't look like I thought you would. Uniform and all."

Jim turned to face him as he opened the door, saying, "And you're pretty much the same as I imagined. But, come on in any way.

Have a seat," Jim told them as he headed to the bedroom. "I'll be right back as soon as I can get rid of the *uniform* and try to match whatever image I'm supposed to live up to."

When Jim came out a couple of minutes later in a pair of Wranglers and a T-shirt, Bob stood and apologized, "I didn't mean anything by my comment. I just didn't expect to see an airline pilot. No offense."

"None taken," Jim said, smiling. "I sometimes don't recognize me in the uniform either. If I pass a mirror in the airport, even I think I'm someone else. Beer, anyone?"

"Please," Gene said as they both rose and followed Jim into the kitchen.

After passing around the bottles, Jim said, "Let's go out onto the porch. I've been cooped up in that damn airplane or a hotel room for three days, and I'm ready for some fresh air."

As they took their seats, Jim asked, "Isn't the big guy you sent into that bar coming?"

"No, he just did us a favor by going in with the ladies," Gene explained, setting his beer on the wrought iron table.

"He sort of owed us a favor, but he's not part of the company."

"Do you have a lot of people owing the company favors?" Jim asked, looking at Bob.

"A few," Gene answered. "But we try not to use them unless we have to. It's better to have them in reserve if we can manage without them.

And now that we've been repaid, that particular man is off the hook," Gene finished.

"But knowing that guy, he'll need another favor before too long," Bob replied, smiling. "I'd say that resource will be constantly in our debt."

"Okay," Jim said, looking back at Gene. "What's the latest on Robertson, and do you guys have any tentative plans that we can enact in the four days I have off?"

"The latest *tentative* plan is for Bob to get Jack to agree to make the hit," Gene told him. "That part isn't really much developed, except that we need to get him on tape saying that he shot David. And we'll also be recording everything he says when he actually makes the *hit*."

"How do you plan on doing that?" Jim asked Bob.

"I'll go back to the bar and get him to come over to my table," Bob explained. "I'll be with the same two ladies, and I'm sure he'll agree to do anything to impress them, as well as me.

If he doesn't want to talk in front of them, I'll have them go sit at the bar until we finish our conversation," he continued. "Once I have his recording, I'll explain the setup."

"I think we need to have our man in the Dallas Police Department meet with us," Jim said. "I don't want some patrol car coming up when we do this unless we know who's driving it."

"He'll be here tomorrow," Gene told him. "He couldn't get off today. This meeting is just for you to meet Bob in case we need him to be with Jack. I don't want you mistaking him for one of Jack's friends."

"And I damn sure don't want to be shot," Bob said, picking up his half-empty beer. "And I wanted to get a feel for you. It's my ass hanging out there. I'm sure you understand.

I'm trying to decide if I need to be with Robertson or not when you arrange this traffic stop or whatever you eventually decide to go with," he continued. "There are so many things that can go wrong if I'm in that car."

Jim sat looking at Bob for a moment and then got up, saying, "I think we'll need a couple of more beers before we go any further."

Chapter Sixty-Four

"Okay," Jim said, returning with three beers. "Here's what I think. I think Bob needs to be in the car with Jack."

Handing each of them a fresh beer, he continued, "That will give him confidence that some member of the Aryan Circle is watching him and will grant membership if he completes the hit.

And it gives us another gun if things go to shit," he finished as he twisted the top off his Ziegen Bock. "I want to put the bullet through his face, but if that asshole has a gun in his lap when I approach, I'll be happy to give the pleasure to Bob here."

"That would be my pleasure," Bob said, lifting his beer to Jim. "If it was up to me, I'd just take the little prick outside the bar and run an ice pick through his ear."

"I'd say okay to that if it wasn't to help David's family regain some trust in the police," Jim told him. "The way we're planning it gives them more of a feeling of justice."

"Not to mention you've developed a relationship with the family and want to do this for Marie as much, or more, as the rest of the family," Gene added.

"I do," Jim agreed. "Also, I want any asshole who kills an innocent man, or woman, to suffer the same fate."

"Jim's an Old Testament sort of guy," Gene said, looking at Bob. "I won't get into any specifics, but that seems to be his sole religious belief."

"Everyone has their reasons," Bob said, nodding. "I'm having a hard time playing my part with these white supremacist assholes. But, until this is over, my life more or less depends on it."

"Not to bring this up," Jim said, looking at Bob's tattoos, "but what's going to happen to you when it is over? I mean, the tattoos and everyone knowing who you are?"

"The tattoos will disappear," Gene answered. "They're a special dye that we can take care of. We've already had to refurbish them a couple of times to keep the colors right. And Bob, whoever he was, will die in a horrible accident.

The new *Bob* will join his family in Canada or somewhere they decide they want to live," he continued. "This is one of his final assignments before he returns to his normal life."

"Understood," Jim said, nodding and taking a drink of his beer. "What about our police officer? Will he remain with the Dallas Police Department?"

"Yes," Gene answered. "That's his actual job, just as yours is with the airlines. "He'll actually play no part in the plan except to help us get the car and uniform."

"Okay," Jim replied. "When do we do this?"

"Day after tomorrow," Gene told him. "Bob's meeting with Jack tomorrow, and if that goes well, we should be finished by mid-afternoon the next day."

"Have you decided on where?" Jim asked.

"Cedar Crest," Gene answered. "Two reasons. First, it's the most crime-ridden area that Dallas covers. Second, and you'll like this one, it'll be the same intersection where Jack shot David."

"Don't you think that may raise some eyebrows?" Jim asked, looking from Bob to Gene. "Too much of a coincidence?"

"I can take care of that," Bob answered. "That neighborhood is about sixty percent black and over thirty percent Hispanic. That would be the logical place to find a non-white officer.

That's probably why he picked it in the first place," he continued. "And I doubt if he'll remember the exact spot he shot your friend.

To me, it's the perfect spot," Bob finished. "Especially since you're, how did you say it, Old Testament? Sort of fits, doesn't it?"

"Works for me," Jim agreed. "Now, what weapon will you be using?"

"We've managed to get a Smith and Wesson 38 that will be matched to an Aryan Nation shooting in that neighborhood last year," Gene said. "After you've taken care of Jack, Bob will wipe it down and put Jack's prints on the shells and all over the gun. We'll let the Aryan boys try to say he wasn't one of them after it hits the news."

"What about my gun?" Jim asked.

"It's a gun that will match a bullet found in the attempted robbery of a grocery store last year," Gene answered. "And the bullet in Jack's head, or wherever it's found, will be a perfect match. I'll bring it in when I go get the uniform."

"How did you manage to find that gun?" Jim asked.

"Let's just say that sometimes it's necessary to stage something so we can use it to our advantage later," Gene answered, smiling. "You never know when you'll need some evidence to improve your chance of success. Like this operation."

Jim thought for a second and then asked, "Have you ever used someone's gun to *stage* something so you can use his gun against him?"

"I won't say if we have or haven't," Gene told him, "But sometimes the means to the end are important."

"So, then you have," Jim said, nodding and finishing his beer. "When will the car be ready?"

"The patrol car will be dropped off here tomorrow at noon when our officer comes here to meet us," Gene answered.

"He'll go over the car with you to make sure you know how to operate the lights and equipment. Then I'll take him home since he's off for the next two days," he continued. "I'll bring him back here to get his car as soon as you let me know you're home.

Do you have any other questions?" Gene asked, finishing his beer.

"Yeah, do you guys want another beer?" Jim said, getting up. "And yes, I'll probably have more questions tomorrow when we meet again."

Chapter Sixty-Five

After Gene had left with Bob, he decided to call Marie and see what she was doing. As she answered, he simply said, "Hey, how's the house coming?"

"Not too bad," she told him. "Matter of fact, my bedroom is finished. I've got everything back in there, so I can at least spend the night in my own house and sleep in my own bed."

"I know that's a big step," Jim said. "After two or three nights sleeping in hotels, I'm so happy to get home and crawl into my own bed. I don't care how ritzy a hotel is. I prefer my own bed."

"Why is that?" Marie asked. "I mean, a bed is just a mattress, a pillow, sheets, and a blanket or something."

"I think it's that my mattress has changed to accommodate me," Jim answered. "It's found how I like to lay and molded itself. As far as the pillow goes, hotel pillows are always manufactured stuff like rubber or something. I'm so happy to get home and lay my head on a soft goose-down pillow."

"I think a lot of it is the subtle odor from your body," Marie argued. "I mean, if you're in a hotel bed, there's always some lingering odor from strangers.

Good or bad, I swear I can sometimes smell David when I go to bed," Marie added. "Just as I'm sure that's one of the moments you remember, Jennifer."

"You're probably right," Jim agreed. "But you'd think that after a couple of years of washing the sheets, it would disappear."

"You don't wash the mattress," Marie said. "And you don't wash the pillows."

Marie waited a couple of seconds and then said, "Speaking of beds and pillows, since I finally have a bedroom, how would you like to come over and see what I've done? I'll even stock up on that beer you like. What's it called? Oh yeah, Ziegen Bock."

"That sounds good, except that I've already had a couple of those beers I like," Jim answered. "On top of an empty stomach, I don't need to be on the road.

But you're most certainly welcome to come here and join me," he continued. "I'll order one of those delivery pizzas, and I'll come see your remodeled bedroom some other time."

"You'll do no such thing," Marie said, laughing. "Delivery pizza. How dare you?"

"Doesn't your dad have delivery?" Jim asked. "Or at least carry out?"

"Delivery, no," she answered. "Carry out, yes. And I'll call him and bring a carryout. If that's all right with you."

"That sounds great," Jim told her. "I'll jump in the shower as soon as we hang up, and I'll be clean, odor-free when you get here."

"Not to mention that you don't have to have eight hours of uninterrupted sleep tonight," Marie joked. "If I have my way, you may get a *couple* of hours of *uninterrupted* sleep."

"You must be talking about someone much younger than me," Jim replied, laughing. "At my age, the important things in life are a good night's sleep, a good bowel movement the next morning, and doing it in that order."

"You have such a way with words, Mr. Lashley," Marie said, laughing. "I'd think you're heading for one of those retirement villages the way you talk."

"Not that far gone yet," Jim replied. "And not looking forward to that either."

"Then I guess I better hurry over there," Marie said. "Maybe I can delay that gruesome future for a few hours. I'll see you in about an hour."

"I'll leave the door unlocked," Jim said, picking up the Dallas Police Officer uniform and pistol Gene had left.

"What if I'm early?" Marie asked, smiling to herself. "Shall I just walk in? What if you're still in the shower? Shall I join you?"

"I don't think we need to worry about that," Jim answered, laughing. "I'm pretty sure it'll take your dad more than fifteen minutes to make the pizza, and it's at least a twenty-minute drive from the restaurant to here.

If I'm still in the shower after thirty-five minutes, you better call 911," Jim added. "No, I'm pretty sure I'll be fully dressed when you get here."

"Maybe I'll just head that way right now and meet the delivery boy at your house with a pizza I'll order as soon as you hang up," she joked.

"Even I know you'd never order delivery," Jim said, hanging the police uniform in the back of his closet and putting the pistol beneath some sweaters. "Your dad would disown you if he ever found out you'd done that."

"Okay, I guess the shower thing will have to wait," Marie said, trying to sound disappointed. "But I'm sticking with what I said about that worthless eight-hour crap. Not tonight, Mr. Lashley."

Chapter Sixty-Six

The next morning, Marie followed Jim to Denny's for breakfast before heading back to Garland. As she left, Jim stood watching her and waving before getting into his pickup.

As he arrived back at his house, he noticed a Dallas Police patrol car sitting at the curb. After he parked in the driveway, a man wearing a police uniform stepped from the patrol car and headed for him as he got out of the pickup.

"Jim Lashley, I presume," the officer said as he reached Jim.

"Yes, sir," Jim said, offering his hand. "And I'm guessing Gene sent you."

"That he did," the officer said. "By the way, I'm Reggie Simpson."

"Good to meet you, Reggie," Jim said, shaking his hand and turning toward the front door. "Let's get inside and wait for Gene."

"Coffee?" Jim asked as he shut the door behind Reggie.

"No thanks," he answered. "I don't mean to rush you, but I need to get home, so if you don't mind, I'd like to go over the cruiser with you, so I'll be ready to leave when Gene gets here."

"No problem," Jim said. "Let's get that taken care of right now."

Allowing Reggie to lead, he said, "I've had a little experience with some of the basics, but it never hurts to have a refresher course."

"Certainly can't hurt," Reggie said, opening the driver's door. "Why don't you jump in, and I'll give you the nickel tour. Then you can ask any questions about anything you don't understand, or I failed to cover."

Sliding into the seat, Jim took a moment to look around and then touched the control panel for the light bar and emergency system located to the left of the speedometer.

"Looks familiar," Jim said. "Anything unique about this one?"

"Not really," Reggie said, shaking his head. "This is pretty much the same as in every other car I've used in other departments. Sometimes, it's located differently.

Now, you'll notice the radio on the right side," he continued. "It's set on the dispatcher at the DPD, and I'd suggest you leave it there.

At least you'll hear if something is going on around you," he said. "Or worst case, you've been noticed by someone, and they've called you in.

By the way, I've modified the numbers on the sides and top to make sure this car can't be traced to me," Reggie finished as Gene pulled into the driveway and parked behind Jim's pickup. "I'll change them back before I go back to work."

"Reggie, I see you've met Jim," Gene said, walking to the cruiser. "Got any problems here, Jim?"

"Nope," Jim said, getting out of the car. "Pretty standard setup. About the only thing I'll be using are the red and blues pulling one car over."

"Do you have anything for Jim?" Gene asked Reggie. "If not, I'll run you home and come back for you tomorrow afternoon."

"I guess not," Reggie answered, shaking his head. "Jim seems to be familiar enough to run the light system since that's all he anticipates using.

And I'm sure he'll give due diligence in staying within the law when he's driving it," Reggie joked as Jim shut the car door. "And no unauthorized personnel in the front. And definitely no hanky-panky in the rear seat, with or without handcuffs."

"Well, crap," Jim said, laughing. "Now I'll have to call Marie and tell her there's no need to wear her orange jumpsuit for our date tonight.

I had really planned on arresting her and forcing her to admit she was planning some highly erotic activity that is banned in at least thirty-three of the fifty states," Jim continued as Gene stood shaking his head.

"But, in deference to your generosity in letting us use your patrol car, I'll interrogate her in the whips and chains room in my house," Jim finished smiling.

Reggie stood silently for a couple of seconds and then burst out laughing and said, "I think maybe I'll make an exception this one time, but you use your own damn handcuffs!"

"We'll have a beer when you come to get your car," Jim told him, grinning. "Just give me an hour or so to Lysol the rear seat, and I'll leave the windows down, at least the front ones, to let it air out."

Reggie looked at Gene and shook his head, asking, "What the hell did you get me into, General? I thought cops were a little on the crazy side, but …"

Chapter Sixty-Seven

Gene had just gotten out of his car, returning from taking Reggie home, when Bob pulled in behind the patrol car on his Harley.

Having heard the distinct sound of the bike, Jim came out as Gene was shaking Bob's hand. "Nice ride," Jim said, shaking his hand also. "Hard to sneak up on somebody, though."

"I want them to know I'm there," Bob said, smiling. "If you've got it, flaunt it."

"And I was just about to buy a new Lamborghini to show that *I've got it*," Jim said, laughing. "But you've just saved me almost a million dollars. Looks like it's time for another beer."

After gathering three beers, Jim joined Gene and Bob on the back porch and passed them around, saying, "I've been thinking about the gun issue tomorrow.

I'm a little concerned about Jack having a weapon," he explained as he took his seat. "I don't want him to be armed. What's your opinion, Bob?"

"I'm definitely not opposed to that," he answered. "One less chance of me getting shot."

"How do you propose making sure he isn't armed?" Gene asked. "He thinks he's on his way to shoot another police officer."

"I think I can handle that," Bob said, taking a swig of his beer.

"How?" Jim asked, wondering himself.

"I'll just tell him that he's the wheel man," Bob answered, setting his bottle down. "If I get the recording of his shooting that David guy, that's all we really wanted from him, isn't it?

I mean, you're going to off him tomorrow anyway, so why does he need a gun?" he continued. "He isn't going to be charged with another death. Matter of fact, he isn't going to be charged with anything."

Jim looked at Gene, who was slowly nodding and said, "Okay. I'll certainly be a lot happier if he's unarmed. So, let's walk through how this will happen."

For the next hour, they made several tentative plans using every scenario they could think of. Finally looking at each other, Jim announced, "I think we've done about all we can do. As the General is so fond of saying, *Flexibility is the key to success.*"

"And you add that lack of information is the key to flexibility," Gene said, finishing his beer. "And you then postulate that the less you know, the more successful you will be."

"Okay, guys," Bob said, getting up. "You're starting to use words that I've never heard before. So, I'll just head on down to the bar and seduce, a big word I do know, Jack into confessing to shooting a police officer and that he wants to shoot another one."

"Not to be a complete asshole, Bob," Jim said, getting up. "But the word seduce is normally reserved for sexual activity. And I'm pretty sure that isn't the intent here. Perchance, you may mean entice?"

"No," Gene said, laughing. "Entice generally means to give pleasure. Might I propose to convince?"

"Assholes, both of you," Bob said, laughing and shaking his head. "How about I just *convince* the little prick to spill his guts and agree to come unarmed into what he believes is the assassination of a police officer."

"I'm *convinced*," Jim said, laughing. "How about you, General?"

"Definitely *convinced*," Gene said, recalling the dark humor and constant ribbing of each other when on the battlefield.

"I was going to say persuade, but once again, we are shown how language is the greatest miscommunication tool among mankind," he said, laughing.

"Well, then, perchance, we should resort to the first form of communication between men prior to the verbal," Bob said, grinning and displaying the universal sign language of his middle finger pointing in the air.

"I'll give you a call after my meeting at the bar this afternoon," he said, turning to walk away. "Unless something changes, we're still on for twelve o'clock at the corner of Stafford and West Rochelle."

"Sounds good, Bob," Jim said, following him to the front door. "Watch your back around that guy. Anyone so anxious to join any Aryan group that would have him wouldn't hesitate to kill you if he thought it would give him some creds with some other group."

"Not to worry," Bob said, sliding some mirror sunglasses down. "These little puppies give me a rear view. See you tomorrow."

Chapter Sixty-Eight

While Jim and Gene were sitting on the porch going over the latest intelligence from the Galveston operation, Bob rode his bike to the bar and walked in.

Never appearing to look around, he spotted Jack sitting by himself at a table on the left side of the room. Walking without looking his way, Bob saw an empty table on the right side and strolled over there.

Nodding at the bartender, he sat back and waited. A couple of minutes later, the bartender brought him a mug and turned away.

Just after that, the two ladies he had talked to outside before entering walked in and headed straight for Bob's table. As they got there, each hugged his neck and kissed him on the cheek before sitting down.

Bob looked at the bartender again and nodded. Still not looking in Jack's direction, he carried on small talk with the two girls until their beers arrived.

Finally, one of the ladies got up and walked over to where Jack was sitting and said, "Bob wants to talk to you."

As she walked back, Jack swallowed the last of the beer in his mug and followed.

Arriving at his table, he said, "I understand you want to talk to me."

Bob looked up and stared at him for a couple of seconds and then said, "Take a seat."

Jack sat down and looked at Bob for a few moments and then asked, "What did you want to talk about?"

Bob sat looking at him and finally said, "I hear that you shot a cop a couple of years ago."

Jack looked at both ladies and back at Bob before asking, "Where did you hear that?"

Again, Bob took his time looking at him and finally tipped his head back and pointed his chin at the bar.

Both girls got up and started to walk away. As the one to Jack's right passed him, she rubbed her hand across his left shoulder and smiled at him.

As they got out of listening range, Jack asked again, "Where did you hear that?"

Prolonging the silence, Bob finally said, "Word gets around. Now, is it true?"

Jack glanced around and said, "Could be true. Why do you want to know?"

"You're not here to ask questions, dipshit," Bob said, glaring at him. "You're here to give answers.

Now, did you shoot a cop a couple of years ago or not?" Bob said, leaning forward, cupping his hands, and resting his elbows on the table.

Jack leaned back in his chair and finally admitted, "Yeah. I did."

Bob leaned back and said, "Tell me about it."

"What do you want to know?" Jack asked.

"Everything," Bob merely said. "Tell me what happened and why you shot him."

Jack thought about what he would say and finally said, "Me and a friend of mine were cruising an area where we knew we could score a couple of bags of weed and maybe a couple of dime bags of coke.

Anyway, this cop pulls me over for no reason," Jack continues. "He asks for my license, and then I ask him why he pulled me over.

He goes into this BS about how I don't fit the neighborhood and was acting suspicious," Jack explained. "Then he asks where I live and what I was doing there.

So, I tell him I'm there looking for some Beaner that my mother paid a hundred bucks to come clean out her flowerbed," Jack continued.

"Then I told him I was there to find the taco eater and either get my mother's money back or have him jump in the bed of my pickup and take him to do what he promised," Jack added.

"So, the cop says, *"'And where do you live that your mother was here looking for yard work?'*

And I tell him we live on Emmersome Street," Jack said, smiling.

"Then the cop sort of looks off like he's trying to figure out where Emmersome Street is," Jack said, laughing.

"Well, when he looks back, he says, '*I've never heard of Emmersome Street,'*" Jack says, grinning and shaking his head.

"Well, I just raise the 45 I had in my lap, point it at his face saying, '*Emmersome ... as in Emmersome huge huevos you got on you Cochise for pulling me over,'* and I pull the trigger spraying that asshole's brains across the street."

Chapter Sixty-Nine

Bob just sat staring at him and finally reached up and took his sunglasses off saying, "That tracks. Maybe not the bullshit narrative, but the rest of it matches."

"Why did you want to know?" Jack asked, sitting back and thinking about getting another beer.

Again, Bob sat looking at him and finally answered, "I need a little, let's say, something that might be right up your alley,"

Bob looked at him a few seconds before nodding at the bartender as Jack sat wondering where this was leading.

After the bartender brought their beers, Jack asked, "What do you need?"

"I've got a slight issue with a fellow that's been giving some of my people a little problem," Bob told him. "There's one particular patrolman working in the Cedar Crest area that's causing us some financial harm. That has to stop."

"What can I do to help?" Jack asked, thinking that this was his big chance. Not to mention that one of the ladies had shown some interest in him.

"I need a driver," Bob said, leaning over the table. "No guns, no bullshit, just someone who knows how to get things done."

"I'm your man," Jack told him. "I know that area like the back of my hand."

Staring at him for a few moments, Bob finally said, "Okay, here's the deal. You'll pick me up here at ten o'clock tomorrow morning. The man I'm after will be patrolling the area around Stafford Street between ten and twelve.

I want you to drive around until we spot him; then, we'll make a couple of passes," Bob explained. "We'll do something to get him to pull us over, and I'll take it from there."

"You don't want me to just take care of it for you?" Jack asked, thinking that he would be assured entry into the Aryan Circle if he did this for Bob.

"No, this is personal," Bob said, shaking his head. "I don't want you to even have a gun. This is my hit, and I don't want bullets flying like at the battle of Little Big Horn."

"Another tomahawk chunker, is he?" Jack asked. "Why do we have those teepee sleepers telling us white folks what we can do?"

"You want the job; you follow my rules. Understand?" Bob said, glaring at Jack. "No guns. Just drive and do what you're told."

"Got it," Jack said, nodding as he nervously took a swig of his beer. "Drive. Nothing else."

"Exactly," Bob said, motioning for the ladies to return. "What will you be driving?"

"I've got a cherry red 1973 Ford 150 with a rebel flag sunshade on the rear window," he answered proudly as the ladies brought their beers and sat down.

"That should get his attention," Bob said, smiling at him. "Show the flag."

"That's my motto," Jack said, smiling at the girl who had touched his shoulder.

"Good," Bob said as he finished his beer and stood up. "Now, ladies, either drink up or leave it. We've got places to go and people to see."

Outside, Bob thanked them and watched them drive away before jumping on his bike. A couple of blocks away, he stopped at a gas station and pulled out his cell phone.

Waiting until he heard Gene answer, he said, "It's set. He's picking me up here at the bar at ten o'clock tomorrow morning. We should be in the target area by ten thirty."

Listening to Gene for a couple of minutes, he said, "We'll be in a red 1973 Ford 150 with a rebel flag sunscreen on the rear window. It won't be hard to spot. What a dumbass."

Listening again, he said, "Got it. We'll be there."

As Gene hung up, he turned to Jim and said, "That was Bob. It's on. He's meeting Jack at ten and wants to make the hit around ten thirty."

"That's fine," Jim said, getting up. "Another beer?"

"No, but I'm in the mood for some Italian cuisine," he said, finishing his beer. "Think your friends up in Garland will let us grab a bite?"

Chapter Seventy

The next morning, Jim got up early and started his coffee pot, anxious to begin the operation that would bring closure to Marie and her family. Already dressed in the uniform of the Dallas Police Department, he took a cup of steaming brew out to the back porch.

Sitting there enjoying the morning, he inspected the gun for the third time that he would use to remove a cop killer from the streets once and for all.

Satisfied it would perform as expected, he slid it into the holster hanging on his right hip. Running through the plan again, looking for flaws or ways to improve the likelihood of success, he was envisioning walking up to Jack's truck when his phone rang.

"Good morning, Jim," Marie said happily. "How are you planning on spending your day off?"

"I'm going to meet a couple of friends for lunch around noon," he replied. "Other than that, no real plans. Did you have something in mind?"

"Well, the girls are driving down from Denton," she answered. "I told them they need to get their bedrooms put together so we can start living as a family again when they come home.

I've finished mine, so now it's time for them to take care of theirs," she continued. "Seppa suggested that you come to help them, and they'll cook dinner for us. Doesn't that sound like fun?"

"Let me think about that," Jim answered, laughing. "Put the bed up beneath the window. No, move it over to the other wall. No, that's not right either. Put it back under the window and move the chest of drawers to the side opposite the closet.

I can't think of a more *fun* way to spend the afternoon," he said. "Now, the real question is … can the girls cook?"

"Not really," Marie answered. "But they're great at telling me what they want and do a pretty good job of standing around making comments."

"Well, if that's all it takes to be a good cook, count me in," Jim said. "I'm a master at standing around making comments. What time should I be there?"

"The kids will get here around two, so will that work for you?" she replied.

Running the timing of the morning's events through his head, Jim said, "That should work. I'll just need to do a few chores before I have lunch, and then I can hurry back here and take a quick shower. Yeah, that should work just fine."

"What chores are you doing this morning?" Marie asked.

"Just some overdue cleaning, taking out the trash, nothing extraordinary, just stuff that's been put off too long," he answered.

"You probably don't need to take a shower before you come," Marie argued. "You'll be doing manual labor and will probably just need another shower after that."

"I'd rather start clean," Jim said. "And, if I'm not mistaken, you did mention something about joining me in the shower.

Granted, this is your shower instead of mine, but a shower is a shower," he joked. "And by the way, did you notice that *manual labor* has the word 'man'? Why are so many words about what men should do or the problems they cause?

Take the phrase *mental problems*," he continued. "*Men*-tal problems? *Man*-ipulate? *Man*-like?

Okay, manlike is okay. But there are many others, too many to get into right now. Do you think it's fair to blame us, the male gender, for all the world's problems?" he finished.

"Maybe not all *Man*-kind," Marie replied laughing. "But in your case, I think *Men*-tal defect may be appropriate. You come up with the strangest things sometimes. Does your brain ever just hurt from the swirl of unconnected thoughts?"

"Constantly," Jim said, laughing with her. "But I soothe it with a generous dose of Jack Daniel's when it gets too close to imploding."

"I'll try to keep a prescription refilled here," she replied. "Can't have that happen. Besides, I think science would be interested in the inner workings of a tumultuous brain."

"That was unnecessary," Jim said, looking at the time and realizing he needed to get going. "My brain isn't disorganized. It's just that I'm not sure where everything is and have to move stuff around while I'm looking.

But we'll have to finish this most illuminating conversation later," Jim told her. "Perhaps this evening while the girls and I stand around making comments."

"Okay," Marie told him. "You have fun with your chores this morning, and I'll see you around two."

Chapter Seventy-One

Jim had barely gotten off the call when Bob called, saying, "I'm getting ready to go meet Jack. Has anything changed?"

"Not that I know of," Jim answered. "I haven't heard from Gene this morning, but I plan on being at the corner of Stafford and West Rochelle by ten in case you come early."

"That works for me," Bob told him. "My plan is to cruise by you so that I can identify you. Then, I'll have Jack bring us beside you on the next run as we come from behind you.

Since you'll be sitting just back from the stop sign on Rochelle, I'll flip you the finger, and we'll run the stop sign," Bob explained. "We'll head west, and I'll have him pull off just before we get to Story Road.

There's a little access road that leads back toward a big building with a Dollar General and some other crap," he continued. "We'll pull up just as we get to a place called the Express Mart or something like that.

There shouldn't be much, if any, traffic there, so I doubt if anyone will take notice of a routine traffic stop," he said. "Once you pop Jack, I'll get in the rear of the cruiser and stay out of sight until we're clear of the area."

"That sounds good," Jim agreed, realizing that he needed to get going to make sure he was in place when Jack and Bob drove by.

"Not to be overly cautious, but have you considered checking Jack's pickup before you guys leave the bar?" Jim asked. "It's possible he would hide a weapon beneath the seat or somewhere."

"I'll make damn sure that he's clean," Bob said, agreeing. "That little prick is just sneaky enough to try something like that."

Almost immediately after hanging up, Jim's phone rang again, and he answered, "Hello."

"Good morning, Jim," Gene said. "I just wanted to let you know your phone and Bob's were activated this morning, and I heard you discussing the operation ..."

"Then that means you also heard my conversation with Marie," Jim accused him. "Why didn't you let me know my phone was active?"

"Hold on," Gene said. "That was my fault. I should have called you and told you. I didn't. But, as soon as I heard it was Marie, I shut down the speakers.

And I've had all of your conversation removed from the records," he continued. "Again, I apologize and give you my word that nobody here heard that conversation ... nor will they ever hear it."

"This is exactly what I've been afraid of," Jim told him. "And not just for me, for everybody. When some agency can monitor your every word, as your system can, where do we find privacy?

Do I need to start removing the battery from my phone if I have someone over for the evening?" Jim continued. "Where does this stop?

Of course, I'm glad we can use it to catch the bad guy, but who decides who the bad guy is?" Jim complained. "I know it's important, and I appreciate the fact that you can monitor me when I'm on a mission and can tell me where the bad guys are.

But I want the capability to shut this crap down when I'm not actively involved with Black Water," Jim finished. "And I want it now. Not tomorrow. Not next week. Now. Or I'm pulling the battery and leaving this damn phone in a kitchen drawer."

"Are you done?" Gene asked after allowing a few seconds to pass. "If you are, I'll tell you what I instructed Bracer to do this morning when I discovered that your phone had been activated.

I told her to put a system in place before noon today that would allow anyone who worked for Black Water, or its subsidiaries, to have control over when their phones could be activated," he continued. "I told her to prioritize those agents in the field, like you, who only work part-time for the company.

She promised to have it in place no later than three o'clock East Coast time today," he said. "You will be sent a coded message saying you have the option of accepting this modification.

It will give you a four-digit code to enter into your phone," he continued. "It will then give you a few seconds to enter your own code that will block any activation without you entering that code.

Is that sufficient?" Gene then asked. "If it isn't, we'll discuss it after you and Bob take care of the immediate problem. And yes, your phone is still activated."

Chapter Seventy-Two

Jim made sure he had his gun and the keys to the patrol car and announced that he was leaving as he left the house. Hearing a positive response from Black Water, he started the cruiser and pulled from the curb.

"Your target is still with our man where they agreed to meet," the voice of a female told him over his earpiece.

Heading north on 625, he kept his speed exactly at the limit as he watched speeders coming up from behind suddenly slow down to avoid passing him.

Approaching the exit for I 30 West, he turned on his blinker and slid into the right-hand lane. Following the curving road, he soon merged with the traffic heading west on I 30.

Knowing it was about ten miles to where he'd join I 35E northbound, he remained in the left lane until he was forced to move over a lane due to an exit-only sign coming up.

Finally heading north on I-35, he heard Black Water saying that the target was leaving its previous location and was coming north on I-35.

"Distance behind me?" Jim asked, seeing the exit for 183, the east Airport Freeway, a mile ahead.

"Twelve miles," the lady answered.

"Keep me informed," Jim said, sliding into the exit lane on the right.

"I'm probably twenty minutes from the location," he said, heading west on 183, knowing that Bob would be listening. "I should be in position ten minutes before you get here."

Taking the exit for Walton Walker Blvd, he asked, "Distance?"

First, he heard his monitor telling him the target was now only eight miles behind, and then he immediately heard Bob's distinct voice saying, "Slow down, asshole. Do you want to get pulled over? That dumbass cop will still be there an hour from now. And if you screw this up …"

Now assured that Bob would take control of that part of the equation, he could concentrate on appearing as a normal patrol car and watching for Mac Arthur Blvd, which was his next road.

Making the right-hand turn, he knew he was slightly over two miles from his destination. Another half mile, and he'd make a left onto Rochelle.

Shortly after entering MacArthur, he thought about what he had observed driving here. Everybody saw the car, but nobody looked at him. "Well, ain't that something," he said aloud, forgetting about who was listening.

"What?" Gene came on asking. "Is something happening?"

"No, nothing's happening," Jim said, chuckling. "I just thought about something. It's not important. I'll explain over lunch."

Now left on Rochelle, he knew that Stafford would be less than half a mile ahead on the right. Approaching it, he asked, "Distance?"

"Now nine miles," came the answer.

Jim drove past Stafford for a little over a thousand feet until he saw the area where Bob had said they would pull over. Satisfied with the area, he turned around and headed back toward Stafford.

Taking a left on Manion, he followed it to McClure Street. Right on McClure and then right again on Stafford, he stopped just short of the stop sign on Roschelle.

"In position," he said as he checked his pistol one last time.

"Take this right on McArthur," he heard Bob tell Jack. "The guy should be somewhere in this area. We'll follow Rochelle down toward Story Road. He seems to like having lunch at a Schlotzsky's down there."

Moments later, Jim saw a red pickup with two people coming his way. As the pickup slowed down, passing in front of him, he saw Bob and Jack both looking at him.

"That's the asshole," he heard Bob say as they passed. "Take the next right, and we'll come back by him."

Watching until they made the right turn on Manion as he had done, he knew it would only be a couple of minutes until the action would be pitched to a fevered pace.

As predicted and Bob had planned, the red pickup appeared in his rearview mirror. As it pulled up beside him, Bob leaned out the window and gave him the finger.

"Go, go, go," he heard Bob yell as the truck squealed its tires and made a right turn, speeding through the stop sign.

Jim turned on all of his emergency lights and accelerated behind them. Gaining quickly, he heard Bob telling Jack to get ready to pull over.

Seeing them make the turn into the area they had planned, Jim pulled up behind them as they came to a stop beside the Express Mart. Sitting there with his lights on, Jim took a couple of deep breaths and then opened his door.

Chapter Seventy-Three

Jim walked up and stopped just behind Jack's left shoulder and asked, "Going somewhere in a hurry?"

"Why no, officer," Jack said, smirking. "We're just out trying to find somewhere to grab something to eat. No hurry."

"License please, Mr …" Jim asked.

"Robertson, Jack Robertson," Jack replied, leaning over and pulling his wallet from his right rear pocket.

Jim watched him look at Bob expectantly as he sat back up.

Looking at the license, Jim asked, "Does your friend there have any identification?"

"I don't need any identification to ride in a truck, Mister *Police* Man," Bob said, leaning forward so he could see Jim.

"I'll tell you what you do need," Jim said, looking across at Jack. "You need to learn some manners and respect."

"Respect this," Bob said, throwing up both hands with his middle fingers sticking up.

"That's enough," Jim said, stepping slightly back. "You, Jack, put both hands on the wheel and don't move them. And you, whoever you are over there, get out and walk to the front of the truck."

"And why should I do that?" Bob asked as surly as possible.

"Because I asked nicely," Jim said, pulling his pistol out. "Now, please do as I ask.

When you get to the front of the truck, I want you to spread your feet and lean over on the hood with your hands shoulder-width apart," Jim directed as Bob opened the passenger door.

While Jack turned to watch Bob, Jim lifted his pistol and leveled it even with Jack's eyes.

When Jack turned back and saw the pistol pointing between his eyes, he stammered, "What? What did I do? We don't mean no harm. We're just out for some fun."

"You probably don't remember having a little *fun* a couple of years ago, do you?" Jim asked, staring into Jack's eyes.

"A little *fun* shooting a cop about where you saw me sitting?" Jim said, leaning menacingly closer.

"A good cop. A good man. With good children and a good wife," Jim said, putting the barrel of the gun against the bridge of Jack's nose. "Shot him for what? Fun?"

Waiting for a second, Jim continued, "No. It wasn't just for fun. You thought you'd get to join one of those low-life white supremacist groups. And you shot David.

Did you even know his name?" Jim asked, shaking his head. "No? But you saw someone with a darker skin than you, and you decided to prove what a good little white power piece of shit you are.

Well, that good cop. That good man. He was Cherokee," Jim said. "Cherokee. People that were here before flotsam like you drifted ashore. People who had honor, not hatred. People like my grandmother.

Yeah, I'm one of them," Jim said, smiling as he pulled the trigger.

"And now you're dead," he said as he nodded at Bob to put Jack's prints on the gun they had brought.

Moments later, as Bob got in the rear seat of the patrol car, Jim said, "We're done here. Some anonymous person might want to call the Dallas Police and report a shooting.

Of course, they thought the shooters were driving a low-rider Chevy and had bandanas around their heads," he suggested as he turned off the emergency lights and passed Jack's truck.

"Where are you headed now," Gene asked as Jim pulled onto Story Road, heading south.

"Thought we'd grab some lunch," Jim answered, approaching 183 and the West Airport Fwy.

"Any place in particular?" Gene asked.

"I don't care," Jim said as they headed east. "How about you, Bob? Where would you like to go for lunch?"

"I think I saw a Denny's just off 635, somewhere around Town East Blvd," Bob said, laughing. "That sounds good to me."

"Assholes," Gene said. "Both of you. Assholes. Fine, I'll pick up Reggie, and we'll meet you there. Assholes."

Chapter Seventy-Four

When Jim and Bob pulled into the parking lot at Denny's, Jim spotted Gene's black Suburban sitting in the back row. Pulling in beside it, he checked the parking lot before walking with Bob to the entrance.

Once inside, he spotted Gene and Reggie in his uniform sitting toward the rear at a table for six. Stepping up to the table, Jim said, "Reggie, good to see you again. Thanks for the use of your car. I don't think I did any damage, but Bob was in the rear seat.

So, you might want to do that same Lysol thing we discussed earlier," Jim said as he sat across from him and Bob took a chair across from Gene.

"Have you guys ordered?" Jim asked, picking up a menu.

"No, we were being polite and waiting for you," Gene answered. "And why are you looking at a menu? You've probably got it memorized by now."

"Looking at the pictures," Jim said, smiling. "Just looking at the pictures. I swear this picture of a chicken fried steak and eggs looks exactly like the one I'm ordering.

Want to see?" Jim said, holding up the menu for Gene.

"See what I have to put up with," Gene said, looking at Reggie and Bob. "You guys are lucky. You've only had to be around him for a couple of days. I've had to put up with him for more years than I care to mention."

"Ready to order, gentlemen?" a pretty redheaded waitress asked as she walked up to their table.

"Is it too late to get a chicken fried steak with two eggs over medium?" Jim asked, handing her his menu.

"You're just in time, handsome," she said, chewing her gum. "And the rest of you?"

As soon as she had left, Gene looked at Jim and Bob and said, "That was a smooth operation guys. I can't think of a single thing that didn't go as planned. We've received an initial report that a low-rider Chevy was involved, but I believe that will change once the gun you left with Jack is found.

So far, there has been no mention of a Dallas patrol car being at the scene, so that's a big plus," he continued. "I guess we won't know the full story until Dallas analyzes the evidence and they anonymously receive a recording of Jack's admission of shooting David.

That fact alone will probably stop all investigation into his death," he finished. "I doubt if they really care who shot him when they can now confirm that they have the killer who shot one of their officers."

"I'm sure you're right," Reggie said as their orders arrived. "I haven't been on the force with them for very long, but that's pretty much the way things have worked at the other departments I've been with."

"Is Black Water going to share their enhanced imaging process that we used to positively identify Robertson?" Jim asked.

"No, we're not ready to share that capability yet," Gene answered.

"Why not? If it will help clear some cold cases, why not?" Jim asked.

"Because there are other issues. Especially concerning the identification of foreign agents," Gene answered.

"By the way, you were going to explain something over lunch," Gene said, looking at Jim. "Explain."

"Okay, and I'm sure Reggie can back me up on this, but I noticed that people in other cars, especially if they were speeding a little, saw the patrol car but didn't see me," Jim said, looking around. "What I mean is, I watched them slow down, so they obviously knew I was there, but not a soul looked at me when they passed. They must have thought it was one of those self-driving cars."

"That is a fact," Reggie agreed. "I've never had someone passing me look me in the eye. It's like Jim said, I'm invisible."

After everyone had finished and Gene had settled the bill, they walked together to where their cars were parked. As they got there, Gene said, "I'll take Bob home. Reggie, would you mind dropping Jim off at his house?

"I think it would look strange for either Bob or I to be in the cruiser," he explained, smiling. "So, if that's all right with everyone, I'll be in touch in a day or so when I have more information. Until then, again, a great job. I wish they could all go so smoothly."

Chapter Seventy-Five

After giving Reggie back the uniform he had borrowed, Jim took a quick shower and checked the time. Just enough to get to Marie's house if the traffic wasn't too bad.

Calling her as he walked out to his pickup, he asked, "Still need help getting the girls' rooms ready?"

"Of course," Marie answered. "I told them to go make sure they knew where they wanted everything because we didn't want to spend the day moving the same piece of furniture back and forth."

"Yeah," Jim said, smiling as he got in the truck. "As if that'll work."

"Best I can do," Marie replied. "When will you get here?"

"You said around two, so I'll get there around two," Jim answered, starting the truck. "I'm leaving now."

For the next five hours, Jim helped Marie and the twins rearrange their bedroom furniture, take clothes out of boxes, and hang pictures. When they finally finished, Jim asked, "Now that that's done, for the fiftieth and *final* time, what's for dinner?"

"Dad called and said we're supposed to go over there," Marie told him. "And the girls are going back to Denton after that."

"I thought you guys were going to stay here tonight," Jim said, looking at both of them. "Something about needing help getting your rooms ready so you could?"

"We sort of forgot about a little party this evening at the college," Seppa said. "But we're glad you came and helped us. We'll be coming home this weekend now that it's done."

"Yeah," Julie said, smiling sweetly. "We're really glad. We couldn't have done it without you."

"Well, it's no problem," Jim told them. "My gym membership has expired, and I needed a good workout, so I'm glad you let me come over and lift heavy stuff."

"Okay," Marie said, shaking her head. "You two take your car, and I'll ride with Jim. Dad was expecting us thirty minutes ago."

After getting to the restaurant and gathering around the table where they had sat when Gene was with them, Anthony came and took Marie and Jim into the kitchen.

"Listen," he said as he looked around. "I got a call this afternoon from a friend of mine with the Dallas police. Do you remember him, Marie, Matteo DeLuca? Matty?

Anyway, they think they've found the man that shot David," he told them. "Please, don't say anything to your mother yet. I want to be sure before I put her through this again."

"How did they find him, and how do they know it's him?" Marie asked with a look of surprise on her face. "I mean, it's been two years and nothing."

"Matty didn't have all of the details," Anthony said. "Just that the guy they think killed our David was found shot down in Cedar Crest."

"That's where David was shot," Marie said excitedly.

"I know, dear, I know," Anthony said, putting his arms around her. "And this guy is someone they had suspected by couldn't prove anything."

"I'll be so glad if it's really him," she said, shaking her head. "I've dreamed of this day ever since David died. Someone had to pay."

"Let's not get our hopes too high," Anthony cautioned. "There's some other stuff that they think proves he's the guy, but they can't say anything yet.

Someone sent them a tape or something of this guy saying he was the one who shot David," Anthony told her.

"Matty says they'll release the news about the shooting but not about his connection to David until they have verified everything," he said as Marie stepped back and stood beside Jim.

"When will they know for sure?" she asked.

"Matty said probably not for a few days," he answered. "They want to be absolutely positive before they close the case on a cop killer."

"I want to tell the kids," Marie said. "I don't care if it's not positive yet. They deserve to know."

"Please think about it," Anthony pleaded. "They've been disappointed so many times, just like your mother. Please, let's just wait a few more days."

"Okay, Papa," she said, hugging him and putting her head on his chest. "But I want to know the second Matty tells you it was him. The very second."

"You know I will, sweetheart. You know I will," Anthony said, laying his head on hers. "We've both been waiting for this day to come. Now, you guys go join the girls, and I'll be right out with your dinners.

Then I'll come join you for a cautionary celebration," he said, looking down at Marie and up at Jim. "And Jim, I'm glad you're here to support my baby."

"I'm happy to, Anthony," Jim said. "I know how important it is to see justice done when a loved one is hurt."

"I know; Marie told me about your wife," Anthony said, following them out of the kitchen. "That's why I wanted you to be here with Marie when I told her. You know what it's like to have to wait to get justice."

"Yes, sir. I certainly do," Jim replied as they walked to where the twins were sitting and talking to Aurora. "You feel so helpless when you can't do anything."

Later that evening, after dinner was over, the twins had left for Denton, and Anthony had provided the third bottle of wine; Aurora said, "Okay, Tony, just what is it we're celebrating? You never bring out three bottles."

Anthony looked at Marie, smiling, and said, "Our daughter is finally moving out of our house again. Now, I can chase you all over the house naked like I used to years ago."

"Papa!" Marie whispered. "People will hear you! I heard you, and I certainly didn't need to hear that!"

"Not in front of our guests!" Aurora said, slapping his shoulder. "What will Jim think?"

"He'll think that I'm still a man who loves his woman," Anthony said, kissing her. "And I hope these two are with someone they want to chase around the house when they're our age."

"Speaking of the house," Marie said, putting her napkin on the table. "I need to get back to mine before Papa brings out another bottle."

"And I want to thank you for another wonderful evening," Jim said, getting up. "And the meal? Absolutely *just fine!*"

Anthony let out a hearty laugh and said, "You two get out of here. Maybe next time, I'll make you something that is a little better than *just fine*! Go on now. Get out of here."

After getting back to Marie's, they walked in, and Jim put his arms around her, saying, "I think I'll just head on home. You probably need some time alone after hearing that David's killer has been shot."

"No, what I need is for someone to make love to me and hold me all night," she told him, putting her arms around his neck. "Someone who's been through this. Someone who will understand that maybe now I can completely let go."

Pulling Jim's head down, she kissed him and whispered, "Someone like you."

Chapter Seventy-Six

Jim was home shortly before noon, getting ready for his upcoming trip with America when his doorbell rang. Walking from the bedroom through the house, he wondered who would be coming by unannounced.

"Good morning, General," he said, surprised at seeing Gene. "What brings you to my part of town today?"

"Just in the neighborhood," Gene answered. "Thought maybe I'd take an old friend to lunch. That is if we can go somewhere besides Denny's."

"I'm willing to go any place where you're buying," Jim said, laughing. "There's a sandwich place not too far from here that I've been meaning to try unless you want more than just a sandwich."

"No, a sandwich is fine with me," Gene told him. "I had a late breakfast with the Dallas Chief of Police at the hotel, and I just need something to last until I get back to Quantico this evening."

"How'd it go with the Chief?" Jim asked, locking the door behind them as they left.

"Good," Gene said as they got in his black Suburban. "I handed him some of the photos Bracer's people developed and then assured him that the 'anonymous' tape he received had been verified with our voice recognition program.

After looking at the various photos and reading the voice analyzation report, he agreed that Jack had been the man who shot David," he continued as they pulled away from Jim's house. "Which way?"

"Take 635 north and look for Town East Blvd," Jim answered. "Then head east. McAlister's will be on your left after a couple of blocks."

"So, is the Dallas Police Department going to close the case?" Jim asked as Gene headed for 635.

"They'll issue a statement in two days," Gene answered. "First, they'll meet with David and Marie's families and then give a press conference where they'll credit the department with working tirelessly to uncover Jack.

Then they'll go on to say that his arrest was imminent when he was shot by someone with connections to one of the white supremacist groups in the area," he continued as they saw the exit for Town East coming up.

"Any mention of anyone spotting a Dallas patrol car in the area?" Jim asked as they took the exit.

"There was one unsubstantiated call," Gene said, looking for McAlister's. "But the Chief said it was left out of the report since they didn't have any cars in the area at the time of the sighting."

"So that wraps it up," Jim said, nodding as Gene parked.

"That it does," Gene said, getting out of the car. "And the Chief said he'd love to have access to the technology *someone* used to identify Jack from the fragments of photos."

"What did you tell him?" Jim asked as they entered the restaurant.

"I just told him to call me personally if he ever needed assistance," Gene said, smiling as they headed to an open table after placing their orders.

"What's the latest on Galveston?" Jim asked after they had taken their seats.

"The DEA briefed the police departments in each of the cities where Gilliad had operations," he answered. "Then they traced numerous local distributors down to the street dealers.

Thank Maria for that. Yellow Brick Road had very extensive and detailed records of transactions and dealers going back to the very beginning," he continued.

"All total, more than two hundred people have been charged," he finished.

"What about the operation in Mexico? Did we disrupt that source?" Jim asked as their lunches arrived.

"Yes," Gene said as he took a spoonful of Chicken Tortilla soup. "But, as with things of this nature, it's only temporary. Someone will step into El Disenos's shoes. There's just too much of a financial incentive not to. I'm afraid as long as there are people who can't handle life without drugs, there'll always be another *Machete* to supply them. Especially when we don't control our borders and ports of entry."

"I guess that's good for Black Water," Jim said as he took a bite of his Rueben sandwich. "A constant need for their services."

"I'm sure the company would rather stick to other areas of our operations instead of trying to solve problems that affect so many innocent people," Gene told him. "As much as the company wants to be profitable, it's never at the expense of the damages done to the victims and their families that come from drug abuse.

No, we'd like to just stick to catching crooked politicians or unscrupulous businessmen," he added, taking a bite of his New Yorker sandwich. "Now, what's happening between you and Marie?"